Last Ch

Bonnie Edwards

This is a work of fiction. Similarities to real people, places, or events are entirely coincidental.

FAKE ME

First edition. May 1, 2023.

Copyright © 2023 Bonnie Edwards.

ISBN: 978-1989226209

Written by Bonnie Edwards.

Table of Contents

Fake Me (Last Chance Beach) 1
Fake Me 3
Chapter One 5
Chapter Two 15
Chapter Three 25
Chapter Four 31
Chapter Five 39
Chapter Six 53
Chapter Seven 59
Chapter Eight 69
Chapter Nine 81
Chapter Ten 89
Chapter Eleven 101
Chapter Twelve 113
Chapter Thirteen 123
Chapter Fourteen 137
Chapter Fifteen 145
Chapter Sixteen 157
Chapter Seventeen 165
Chapter Eighteen 175
Chapter Nineteen 181
Chapter Twenty 193
Chapter Twenty-one 205
Recent and Upcoming Last Chance Beach Titles 221

For Lisa S...who steered me in the right direction. You rock!

and for Ted, Always

This is your sunshiney heroine meets grumpy hero plot and I enjoyed it immensely...Slow burn. Fake relationship. beach romance, summer fling...I enjoyed this book so much.

4½ Stars — The Highland Hussy Blogger/Reviewer at Got Fiction?

The author has crafted a romance with engaging characters who have just the right amount of emotional baggage, conflict, and attraction. You'll keep turning the pages to discover exactly what his fiancée did as well as what molded Farren into the woman she is.

5 Stars—Joan Reeves NYT & USAToday Bestselling Author and Blogger at Slingwords.com

The grumpy boss and fake relationship tropes combine to make a satisfying romance. The meet cute, where Grady is convinced that Farren is not really there for her new business but only because his sister sent her, was a fun twist.

4.5 stars! Singles fest was genius[1] – Romance in her Prime

---

1. https://www.amazon.com/gp/customer-reviews/R1OOLXCK823A6F/ref=cm_cr_dp_d_rvw_ttl?ie=UTF8&ASIN=B097ND7V15

Fake Me

HOW TO FAKE OUT A BUSYBODY matchmaker...fake date the match!

International real estate broker Grady O'Hara, unkempt, miserable, and nursing his battered heart, is holed up in the Landseer Motel in Last Chance Beach.

A first-class grump, Grady's appalled that enthusiastic sprite, Farren Parks wants him to open his motel to single parents looking for love. He suspects his sister has sent Farren to lure him into a romance. Again. The last one ended in disaster.

Farren expects him to tolerate children laughing. *No!* Crowds of happy families? *No!*

He does not want a second chance at life. Or love.

Unless Farren agrees to fake date him to fake out his matchmaking sister...

Grady soon plays handyman, painter, and business advisor to Farren's fledgling business, Singles Fest. The happy squeals of children in the pool doesn't grate on his nerves as he expected. He sees parents making romantic connections that stir his heart.

When an old flame of Farren's arrives, Grady wakes up to another looming loss if she gives her first love a second chance. The rival has brought his adorable kids to the motel. A rival who's clearly looking for a new wife...

Chapter One

MAY 31 – THE LANDSEER Motel, Last Chance Beach

Grady O'Hara liked a bit of meat on a woman. Curves were luscious and soft and deserved his attention. But what he didn't care much for was the look of bossy persistence worn by the fireball standing outside his back door. From where he stood in the shadows in his kitchen, he watched her animated, determined face. He'd seen her curves yesterday, so he focused on her expression today. She pouted, she frowned, she glared at the curtained window in his kitchen door as if her eyes could set it aflame.

This was day three of her determined assault on his privacy. She'd come the first time in the morning before any decent person would arrive, as if she wanted to catch him before he left for the day.

Yesterday, she'd shown up around noon and tried to get him to answer his door while he ate his lunch. Not content with grimacing through the square window in the door, she'd stomped around to the living room window on the other side of the house. The private side that faced away from the motel's center court.

She'd peered in, covering her eyes with her hands to see better. The pose had given him a perfect chance to see her lush shape through the gauzy curtains. She'd been wearing shorts that clung to her round, pert bottom, a bright pink blouse that was tied at her waist, and sand on her legs. She must've walked the beach to the motel. The light dancing off the gold sand had accentuated her perfect calves and ankles.

He'd almost opened the door to her then, but when she rapped on the glass of the window, he'd changed his mind. Besides, a man deserved to have a ham and Swiss cheese on rye in peace.

But today—*today*—she stood in the breezeway pounding enthusiastically on his kitchen door at seven-thirty p.m. *What? Had she smelled the scent of grilled steak and come running like a bloodhound?*

The only woman he knew who was more tenacious and ballsy than this one, was his sister, Delphine. And he avoided her, the Queen of Bossy, like the plague. Not always, of course, but these last weeks, she'd been banished from his life. Totally ghosted, like most of the world. Not that he'd told her, but surely by now she'd gotten the hint. He'd never tell her why. He wasn't cruel, just angry about the way she'd taken a wrecking ball to his life.

Sure, she was his twin and felt a compulsion to take care of him. Born ten minutes earlier, Delphine had always seen herself as the caregiver. Had always been bossy. When their mother had passed in their early teens, Delphine had become unbearable. He'd rebelled. Any fourteen-year-old boy would have. She'd become smothering and his grief had not allowed for it. They'd been prickly with each other ever since.

He blinked away his too-common mental lament and heard the woman hit the door again. Faster this time, a tattoo of sharp rapid knocks.

"Mr. O'Hara, I can see you through the window in the door," the woman called. "Won't you please let me speak with you? I promise I won't bite or try to sell you something." She put the lie to her words by biting her full, red lower lip. Then she brightened as if she'd thought of a new tactic. "I'm not selling religion if that's what you think."

But the booklets in her hand told a different story. If he growled with the right tone, she'd never come back.

Plus, he was curious to see what she wore today. More sand? Maybe wedged between her toes?

He opened the door.

Later, he realized that was his first mistake. His second was looking into her incredible purple eyes. If he'd seen the intriguing color before this, he never would've looked into them up close. As it was, his breath failed.

"THANK GOODNESS, YOU opened your door. I was about to give up," Farren Parks said, as she placed her shoulder on the doorframe so Grady O'Hara couldn't slam his door in her face. She smiled beguilingly. It was her best smile and had gotten her out of her share of scrapes in her youth. It worked exceptionally well on men, her brothers in particular. And she should know because she had three.

Delphine, Grady's energetic sister, had told her Grady had gone to ground and no one had seen him in months. Which might work to her advantage. Lonely men could be chatty and the more she got him to talk, the better. Because if he talked, he'd have to listen, too. That's how conversation worked.

Both heavy eyebrows rose as he noticed her lean into his space. His eyes were stormy ocean blue. Appealing in a way. She dismissed her wayward thought. The man was a mess, emotionally and physically. And she had to get inside his house. Inside his head.

If she could make him listen for a few minutes, she could make him love her plans for The Landseer Motel. She'd shown up for three days trying to get him to talk to her, and this was the closest she'd gotten to him. She wasn't about to let a grumpy recluse get in the way of her plans, so she batted her eyes at him for good measure.

She knew the power of her eyes. The color was striking and most people who looked this deeply into them noticed. What she didn't expect was her reaction to his interested study of them. Rearing back didn't break his stare.

She was in battle with a master. He used his intense glare the way she used her eye color and her smile. They were in a stand-off she had no intention of losing.

Clearly, Grady O'Hara glared to take adversaries off-guard, while she used her eyes to entice and get her own way. Two sides of the same coin. She gave herself a mental shake and leaned in closer. Batted her lashes again. Smiled more deeply. Coaxed with a tilt of her head.

She would not fail. If she backed down now or ran like a coward, Singles Fest was doomed. Well, that might be harsh, but her fledgling business would take much longer to take off, and she'd have to reconfigure her plans and budgets. *Not going to happen.*

Delphine had convinced her she needed The Landseer and Mr. O'Hara onboard for Singles Fest to succeed. Without the motel to work with, her ideal, perfect plans for Last Chance Beach's Singles Fest would never pan out. She'd be broke and likely, homeless. At the very least, sofa surfing with one brother and the next. *Ugh.* Wouldn't that be a bunch of I-told-you-sos.

Maybe she shouldn't have quit her job, after all.

"Please, give me half an hour and your life will change."

"Who says I want to change it?" His voice was rough. As if he hadn't used it much. Maybe he hadn't. He'd been locked away inside the Landseer for months. Ever since his fiancée's death.

She sidled a couple more inches through the door. If he slammed it now, it would border on assault. And it would hurt. A lot.

He didn't look like an assaulter, if that was even a word. And Delphine would've warned her if her brother had violent tendencies. She hoped. But her shoulder would take the brunt of the slam and she liked her shoulder just as it was; functional.

Breathe, Farren. He's just a man. A grumpy, grieving man, but still...he was as close to a widower as a man could be and that was all-important. Grady O'Hara held the key to her success. All she had to do was convince him to open a closed motel, step out of his self-imposed exile, and rejoin the world. All in time for a launch of her new enterprise on the Fourth of July. She smiled wider.

"You really should hear me out," she said reasonably. "If only to keep your sister happy."

His startling blue eyes widened, and he opened his mouth as if to yell at her. She ducked inside before he could shut the door on her shoulder.

He spun to track her movements as she stepped into his sanctum. It was all so ordinary, it felt anti-climactic to be inside. She'd expected...a total mess? Maybe a little hermit-like hoarding? But the kitchen was neat, clean, and sported shiny new appliances. Expensive ones. The kind with fancy features any cook would love.

"Delphine," he blustered. "I should've known she'd be behind a woman battering down my door for three days." He rounded on Farren, big and bristly and bearlike. He had broad shoulders—the heavy kind—not the perfect ones on professional athletes. These were the shoulders of a carnival strongman who could lift women and toss them through the air.

Still, even big, brawny, grumps deserved to be happy and Farren was just the girl to sort him out. All she needed was five minutes of his time.

"Ten minutes." She held up all her fingers and bit her lip. His glance swept her face, but he didn't kick her out. Which was something. "Twenty at the most." She flashed her fingers a second time in case he needed help counting.

"I'm an event organizer," she went on. "I used to do the weddings and conferences and other events at the Sands, and I have a plan for The Landseer Motel that you'll want to hear about."

He loomed over her. "No."

She took a step back which took her farther from the door. She glanced through the kitchen into the living area. It was tidy in there, too. And as with the kitchen appliances, a new behemoth of a television hung on the wall. The man liked big and shiny and bells and whistles.

"Please, hear me out," she said as she batted her lashes at him. She quit when she realized how often she'd done it. "The Landseer is perfect in so many ways. Aren't you curious about what I can do with it?"

She raised her palms as if she held the fate of the world in them. That's how it felt to her. Her whole future hung in the balance.

"I'm not curious in the least if my sister has a vested interest in *you* being here." He flicked his gaze from the top of her head down to her sandals. She'd opted to drive today rather than walk the beach, so her feet were sand-free for once. "If Delphine sent *you*, I guarantee there's an ulterior motive, no matter what she told *you*."

The way he said *you*, made Farren's back straighten. He made it sound as if Farren was the worst person in town. And she knew for a fact, she wasn't. She was kind, generally had a happy attitude, and was friendly. She cared about people. Cared about making them happy, too. Cared about lots of things.

That didn't make her a bad person, it made her a good person. But she couldn't tell him that, she'd have to show him.

So, she smiled kindly, the way she did at little children. His shirt had once been meant to wear with a jacket and tie but hung open because half the buttons were missing. It was light blue with a small tan check and because he couldn't button it, gave her intriguing glimpses of a vee of hair on his chest. Very distracting.

"I'm confused by your focus on Delphine," she began again, aiming her gaze away from the man's chest hair. "I can't see what ulterior motive she could have. Your sister's my friend and thinks my plan is great." Maybe them being friends was a stretch, but still, they were acquainted and had chatted several times. Delphine had been the one to pursue the relationship.

Farren had kept it professional until that night last week when Delphine had bought her two glasses of wine in the hotel bar, when her limit was one. That had been the start of a three-hour gabfest that ended with Delphine's insistence that Farren come here to meet Grady.

"She encouraged me to see you, knowing how much you'd want to hear about my plan."

He nodded and slammed his large hands to his hips. "Of course, she did. My sister thinks you're my type. Soft, lush in all the right places. Pretty and earnest." His eyes bored into hers while she wrapped her head around the sharp left the conversation had taken. "She thinks it's time I go back to New York and work from the office. Rejoin the world."

"What are you saying?" Shocked, Farren's mind stalled and got hung up on the "pretty and earnest" part of what he'd said.

"She's matchmaking." He spoke bluntly, then scrubbed a hand across his jaw as if his beard itched. Maybe it did. She didn't want to look too closely in case he had food in it. "She thinks if you showed up here with whatever cockamamie idea you're peddling that I'll be overcome with lust and fall in with your plans."

"Lust?" She backed up again, her gaze darting for another exit or a weapon to use if necessary. She clutched her purse to her chest. Inside was a tablet, heavy enough to startle him with a solid whack. If she clunked him on the head with it, she could probably get out the door.

But maybe that's what he wanted; her running out like a coward. She squared her shoulders.

"She sent me here to tell you about Singles Fest and how The Landseer would be perfect for my plan. None of this"—she waved a hand back and forth between their bodies— "has anything to do with, um, dating?"

He snorted. "Isn't that what I just said? That you have a plan? That she sent you? *Here*. To my house." Had he leaned closer? She stepped back just in case.

"Yes, but..." she trailed off, suddenly unsure. "She told me you needed to hear about—that you'd be receptive to—me." She covered her mouth with her hand, appalled at this now-obvious ploy. "I quit my job for this," she half-moaned to herself.

"Delphine's good, you gotta give her that," he said with a shrug. His gaze sharpened. "You quit your job?"

She nodded, reeling from the enormity of her misstep. Delphine knew that she had quit and had sent her here, knowing full well Grady wouldn't be interested in her ambitious plans. He wasn't "scouting" for new ideas.

"I heard what I wanted to hear," she muttered. She looked into his eyes. They glittered as he watched the light dawn on her face. "She said that you'd be receptive to a business opportunity. She *said* you were looking for new ways to make money." Farren had been desperate to leave her going-nowhere job and launch her own dating app and business. "Are you working from here?"

He nodded.

"But you're not looking for new opportunity."

He stood silent and brooded.

She closed her eyes against the truth. She'd been taken in by her desire to succeed and had ignored all common sense. She could see it now. O'Hara Enterprises dealt in international real estate, not financing start-ups. But Delphine...

"You're a busy man," she said on a hollow whisper. Just because he'd hidden away in Last Chance Beach didn't mean he was a lost soul. Grieving, yes. Lost, no. "I'm sorry to have bothered you."

Farren gathered the little dignity she had left and turned toward the door to leave. She hoped she could make it outside before her stomach rebelled all over the floor. How embarrassing. She'd stormed into a grieving man's home determined to get her own way. To further her own ambitions without a care about what he was going through. She felt lower than a worm.

She reached for the doorknob but long, blunt-tipped fingers held the door firmly shut. He had very muscular forearms and the hair there was on the blond side of brown.

"If my sister talked you into quitting your job, then you should at least get to do what you came for." His voice held six levels of grudge and she could tell it cost him to issue the invitation.

"I had no idea you and Delphine were at odds. She seemed genuinely interested in your welfare and convinced me you'd love this idea." A niggle waffled through her mind. Maybe what Delphine had really said was that Grady was going to love *her*. In her wine-addled head, Farren had taken that to mean he'd love her *idea*. Her belly did another swoop. "I should never drink more than my limit of wine."

He cocked an eyebrow at her non sequitur. She did not come here to be set up with this man.

"Talk to me," he said. "I'll hear you. And I won't serve you any wine." Humor danced in his eyes. "Not if you're a lightweight."

"Seriously? You want to hear about my plans?" she asked as she narrowed her gaze. Suspicion curled through her vitals.

"What else would I be interested in?" he asked silkily. His brows knit and the hairs there stood on end, making them look like caterpillars. The man had been a recluse too long. Basic barbering had been ignored.

Lust came to mind, but she didn't say it. She rolled her shoulders to loosen them. "I think I need to sit down. There's more going on here than I was prepared for."

"That's Delphine for you. The Machiavelli family had nothing on her." He indicated the living room area. Small, neat, and cozy. Decorated in early bachelor, with a futon for a sofa and one solid deep brown leather lounge chair that sat directly in front of the monstrous television.

"To be clear, I didn't quit my job because of Delphine. There were other factors."

His only response was a shrug. "It's done now. You've got a lot at stake."

Was that a coffee table against the wall with one corner held up by decorative pavers? Yes. This wasn't early bachelor; it was college kid décor. But clean, like the kitchen. All the important pieces were new. He had all the luxury a man alone could need.

She cleared her throat and perched on the edge of the futon. The mattress was thin and lumpy, and the frame edge felt hard beneath her bottom. She was afraid if she sat back, the whole thing would sag, and she wouldn't get out again without him tugging her to her feet.

And she really didn't want to hold this man's hand.

She glanced around the rest of the room. A long dead plant stood in the corner, dry as corn husks in October. He tracked her gaze. "It was my great-aunt's plant and I've been watering it, but I think I got here too late."

She gave him a weak smile. Her interest in sharing her business plan had waned. He'd laugh at her, Mr. Big Real Estate guy. O'Hara Enterprises brokered international projects and property.

"You talk, I'll listen," he said as he settled himself in the lounger. He popped up the footrest and folded his hands over his flat belly. He watched her for a moment and then waved his hand like Caesar sending Christians to the lions, urging her to say something.

Still stunned that she was unemployed and staring at the walls that Grady O'Hara had erected around himself, she couldn't think where to start. While she hesitated, he took pity on her.

"Delphine's persuasive," he said not unkindly, "but you don't strike me as the type to quit your job without good reason. And my sister's not so cruel as to convince someone to give up their livelihood. Why not begin with what drove you to leap into the unknown?"

Chapter Two

GRADY HAD TO HAND IT to Delphine, she'd picked an interesting one this time. And if he had to guess, he'd say this Farren Parks had no idea she'd been set up. At least not when she'd been pounding on his door. But now? She was catching on.

He read dawning understanding in her nervous glances and in the way she focused on something over his left shoulder. Meeting his gaze had become impossible and she was taking a long time to answer his question about her leap into the unknown.

Farren looked nervous enough to make a dash for the door, so he attempted a smile to put her at ease. Her startled reaction to seeing his mouth curl up at the ends, put an end to that. Smiling had never been his strong suit. He just wasn't good at it. Add to that he was rusty. Hadn't smiled since his wedding rehearsal dinner.

And hadn't had a reason to smile since.

"Why not start with the idea you have for my motel? We'll go from there." He kept his gaze north of her curves.

Her purply-blue eyes slowed to a stroll as they swept by his face. She was cataloguing him as he'd done through the windows with her for the last three days. He wondered what she saw. He hadn't looked in a mirror in weeks.

She scrutinized his face but didn't lock onto his gaze. Fair enough. Not everyone felt comfortable linking eyes during a business presentation. Women especially. They worried it looked too inviting. That's what Veronica had told him. But his fiancée had told him lots of things. Now, he discounted most of it.

"Yes, yes, the motel. That's the best place to start." Farren cleared her throat and threw back her softly rounded shoulders, like a schoolgirl reading her book report to the class.

He'd hated doing that.

"Would a glass of water help?" he offered.

"It would," she replied through a grateful sigh. "I was excited to present this idea to you and now I'm questioning everything."

"Me, too," he murmured. He rose to get her water and then spoke from the fridge as he held the glass to the water dispenser. "Don't question yourself at this point, not about all the work you've put into this plan of yours. You're here, so you might as well tell me." He'd give her a few minutes to make her case, then let her down gently.

Delphine had missed the mark by a mile with Farren. He and she would never suit. He preferred confident women, not wilting flowers who scared easily, no matter how pretty they were. He frowned to himself. He'd thought of Farren as having a bossy persistence in her expression through the window. What was that if not confidence?

"Don't let Delphine's machinations stick in your head. Her matchmaking has nothing to do with your plans for my motel. Keep to the plan and I'll listen."

He had no idea why he reassured her, or helped her get over her awkwardness, but this mess of an evening was on Delphine, not Farren. It would be cruel to make Farren suffer for his sister's schemes.

"Thank you," she said as she took the glass of water from him. She was careful not to brush his fingers. *Good.* She wasn't looking to manufacture false intimacy where he felt nothing but curiosity. Knowing Delphine's penchant for research, Farren was likely single, available, educated, and from a good family. She'd have to be to suit Delphine's pre-requisites.

Still, Farren wasn't here to drag him into a romance. That was a refreshing change.

Farren took a long drink and then settled the glass on the broad pine arm of the ancient futon. She gave him the same forced smile he'd tried on her. Her lips lifted like a snarling dog's, and he held back a chuckle. She was no better at forced smiles than he was. Her natural one was a killer, though. Blistering to a man who'd been alone for months.

She cleared her throat after she gave up on the half-snarl, half-tooth exam. "Singles Fest."

"Singles what?"

"I'm sorry you think so poorly of your sister's matchmaking, but that's exactly the basis of my plan. Matchmaking. That's why this conversation feels so awkward. Your mind has gone to personal matches, while I'm all about the business of matching other people." She let her gaze find the end of her knees while he struggled to take in what she'd said.

She peeped her pretty eyes at him from under her brows. He lifted his chin at her in a "go on" gesture. But a sick inkling trickled down his spine. His matchmaking sister had sent him a matchmaker. Hadn't Delphine done enough already? Even if she didn't know what he knew about his fiancée, Delphine had to be stopped.

"I work, er, used to work as an event coordinator at the Sands Hotel. I made sure all the weddings went off without a hitch, and that all conferences had plenty of water and tea and coffee for their attendees."

"Logistics."

She nodded. "Sort of. I got supplies to the right place at the right time. Chairs, tables, water, flowers. It wasn't the most glamorous job, but I liked it well enough. And most jobs here rely on tourism." She blinked twice. "And I was good at it. Really good."

"Okay, you have a background in event planning and are organized." He tried to sound encouraging, so she'd relax and get through this dreary presentation faster.

"Yes. I'm organized." She clasped her hands in her lap and looked at him, engaged with her topic, her enthusiasm allowing her to catch his eye. She looked shy, suddenly, and excited. Stunningly beautiful, really, with her wavy black hair and gorgeous eyes.

"I noticed how often single people found themselves in the bar alone, or with other singles, looking to meet someone. For instance, weddings are full of matches struggling to be made. Most of the time the people who were looking found someone. For the night or maybe longer." She waved her thoughts on that away with dancing fingers. "The ones who failed to connect were single parents."

"You can tell when someone at a wedding is a single parent?"

She looked at the ceiling in recollection. When her gaze found his again, she was earnest. "Not at first, I couldn't, but eventually, I developed a sense about them. They tended to be closer to thirty or forty than twenty. Their party clothes are generally five or so years out of date. Once children come along, I guess it's hard to keep up with the newest fashion trends."

"Okay. I have to give it to you, not everyone would notice the nuances." Her skills of observation had been honed. Understanding what people want was a skill that couldn't be taught. She wanted to help people find the right life partner. Her skillset had identified a niche market and the entrepreneur in her wanted to fill it.

His matchmaking sister had set him up with a *matchmaker*. Worse, one who believed this was her life's mission. A couple of blistering epithets winged through his head. But he nodded calmly and hoped Delphine's affairs were in order because her life expectancy had just crashed to nil.

And when she was gone, he'd call dibs on Gramps's classic T-bird if she hadn't willed it to some other member of the family. She didn't deserve it, anyway, especially not after she'd had it painted pink.

"Last year," Farren continued, pulling him back to the present. "I became obsessed with the idea of hosting a festival celebrating single parenthood. There are singles cruises for people who can afford them. There are singles dining clubs for people who want to make new friends or enjoy restaurant meals with others. And let's not mention all the dating apps there are. Why not offer family-oriented inexpensive short holidays or long weekends that focus on single parents?"

He glommed onto one word.

"Inexpensive." He sighed as understanding dawned. "Let me guess. That's where my motel comes in?" He hadn't bothered opening the place since he'd inherited it months ago. He didn't need or want people coming and going and making work. He didn't want to hear the screeches of happy children or splashing in the pool.

Or laughter.

He was busy running O'Hara Enterprises and had more than enough to do every day. Especially since he no longer had an assistant or a sister to help. He'd disowned Delphine last month when the truth had come out. She didn't know she'd been disowned, because he wasn't talking to her, but she'd figure it out soon. Delphine pretended that because they were twins, they had a deeper connection than regular siblings.

But being different genders, meant different eggs. Meant no deeper twin connection. The only thing it really meant was she'd been kicking him in the backside since before birth. He loved her. Of course he did. She was his sister. His first playmate, first friend. His competition for time and attention from their parents. His first confidant. But her interference had to stop.

But Farren was still talking. She'd talked over him as if he hadn't asked where his motel came into her plan. As if she hadn't heard him.

Time to end things so he could go back to whatever the hell he'd been doing before she forced her way inside. He rubbed his hand over his head and noticed how shaggy his hair had become while he'd been holed up.

"You have the largest swimming pool on the island and the biggest playground, too," she was saying. "Your great-aunt loved children and this motel was full of families because she catered to them. It's been years since the motel was at full capacity, but it's a jewel to me."

"You remember Aunt Ellen?" He'd enjoyed seeing the flamboyant woman he'd once called a charming renegade. She'd quoted him in her will when she'd left him the motel. Who knew such a small thing would result in him having this perfect bolt hole?

Farren smiled, and this time, it was a natural glowing grin that lit her face. He took the punch to the solar plexus like a champ. Then he glowered at her for making him feel something.

"Yes," she said brightly. "I remember her. I knew her when I was a child." She flushed. "I'm one of the few people in town who can say I was born and raised in Last Chance Beach. There aren't many of us around." She spoke as if growing up was a rarity and staying in a pokey little beach town an accomplishment.

He cocked his head trying to appear interested. He wondered what she'd be proud of next. Sitting? Dressing herself?

"Most of the people I grew up with have left for better jobs and opportunities." A cloud passed over her face, but she rallied immediately. "I see Last Chance Beach as the best place to live and work. I'm determined to make my own opportunity. I have faith I can do this. Last Chance Beach is enjoying a revitalization and I want to be part of it with your motel."

"Very commendable. But no." He rose to his full height, hoping she'd follow suit and get the hint to leave.

She didn't. She sat there, on the edge of the futon looking up at him as if he should care. He sighed, expelling the air with a low growl.

Heaven help him, she was stubborn. He'd seen the persistence in her face when she'd been pounding on his door. What was that saying? When someone shows you who they really are, believe them.

He should have believed.

FARREN HAD BEEN WARNED how much of a grump Grady O'Hara was. Delphine had made that perfectly clear, so when Grady tried to get her to stand up, she stayed seated. He'd have to pry her out of this futon. Farren was not a pushover, no matter how fierce looking the pusher was. She raised her chin and kept on talking. He'd invited her to tell him her plan, so that's what she'd do.

She was almost as good at talking as she was at organizing events.

"You asked if I remember your great-aunt." She waved him toward his lounger again. "She gave me my first job. I did housekeeping here as a teen, so I'm in the unique position of knowing what goes into the day-to-day running of a motel." She drew in a deep breath and held up a hand, so he'd know there was more.

He sank back down into the lounger. She was convinced that a scowl was his resting face. How sad. Grady O'Hara was a morose, lonely man who seemed to want to stay that way. Surely, he'd been happy before the tragedy.

She couldn't afford to be sidetracked by sympathy for him. Her plan for the motel maybe exactly the thing to help get him out of his funk. But only if he was ready, her inner voice said. No one could predict how long or how deeply a person would grieve.

Delphine had said Grady's business was suffering without his presence in New York. She'd intimated that he'd practically cut her out of his life. That was surely a bad sign. And given his appearance, his situation could be dire.

"The Landseer is the perfect place for budget-conscious single parents to bring their children," she explained. "I have a daycare provider lined up for evenings when I plan adult-only activities. I want a nice mix of adult time and family-oriented outings. Singles Fest can take off. By next year word-of-mouth alone will bring in more people. My rates are low, the motel would be bargain-priced and—."

"Hold it right there," he interrupted, sounding reasonable which didn't hold with the actual words he used.

But, whatever. The grump had something to say so she closed her mouth and waited.

"You want me to re-open a long-closed motel in order to turn it into the bargain store of lodgings in the best up-and-coming beach town in the state?" His fake curiosity made her grind her teeth.

"The Landseer hasn't been closed for that long. A handful of months. Besides, I'll help you myself. Scrub on my hands and knees if I have to." Nothing she hadn't done before.

"I'd like to see that," he muttered. Then he caught himself and frowned. "What does my sister have to do with this?"

He settled more comfortably in his lounger and clasped his large hands over his waist. Farren allowed a sigh of relief.

Clearly, she'd won this skirmish, but she squirmed inside at his flat tone. Not that she'd let him see how uncomfortable he made her. His question ricocheted inside her head. What *did* Delphine have to do with this? His sister hadn't invested a dime. She hadn't offered guidance or business advice. She'd only convinced Farren to come here to talk Grady into letting her use his motel.

"She told me where I could find you," she offered after a moment. *Lame. As if she couldn't track down a man with Grady O'Hara's public profile. Wealthy, handsome-to-some-women*—not her—*grieving men were not like pebbles on a beach.* They were rare and stood out, especially in a town the size of Last Chance Beach. The way he'd lost his fiancée was tragic by anyone's standards. The man was hurting, lost, mourning and here she was chattering about setting people up. Talking about people finding love when he'd lost his own not long ago.

She was all kinds of awful. She sagged in despair at her obstinate behavior. But before she could apologize, he spoke again.

"Of course, she told you how to find me," he replied drily. "My sister has a habit of sending women my way. Or, at least, she used to. I thought she'd have given up by now, considering how things went last time."

Ridiculous. No sister would do something so conniving when the whole world knew Grady O'Hara's beautiful fiancée had drowned the night before their wedding in a tragic canoeing accident. He'd arrived in Last Chance Beach immediately after the investigation into her drowning. The conclusion had been that drinking and boating without a lifejacket could be lethal.

Tragedy had brought this man to his knees. Had made him hide away from life at the Landseer and, as Delphine had explained it, Farren's business plan for the motel was meant to bring him back to life. That was what Delphine had said and now that Farren saw the way he'd let himself go, she agreed. But he wouldn't come back to life through a romantic connection. *No. Never.* And especially not with Farren. She wasn't the type to attract high-powered men.

She was too short, too curvy, too small town. Sure, she had great eyes and black wavy hair, but they could only get a woman so far. Farren could attract men, she just couldn't keep them.

Delphine had spent considerable time talking about how to bring her beloved brother back to life and how Farren's business would convince him it was time to move back to New York and leave the motel in capable hands.

Farren had told Delphine about her housekeeping job at the Landseer and her experience at the Sands. She'd said the motel was the best venue to launch Singles Fest. With Farren's unique understanding of the motel's operation, she'd be able to manage the re-opening. Delphine had been pleased with the perfect match of needs and skills.

"You seriously believe your sister sent me here because she thinks we'd be attracted to each other?" His looks were enough to send most women running into the night. Clearly, he hadn't seen himself in a mirror in months.

He shrugged as if his conclusion was self-evident.

Farren did hold the key to Grady's return to life. He didn't see it yet because he was focused on his sister's romantic interference, rather than Farren appealing to his entrepreneurial spirit. "This isn't what you think it is."

His ocean-dark eyes zeroed in on hers, changing his gaze to predator status. Farren refused to cower and straightened her back.

"Tell me then, what is this about if not Delphine wanting to set us up?" His rough-edged voice softened.

Chapter Three

"YOUR SISTER ISN'T SETTING us up," Farren insisted, but Grady knew better. This poor woman was delusional. He settled into his seat, tossing up the footrest. A quick glance at his feet told him he had a hole in the toe of one sock. Come to think of it, there could be a hole in the sole, too. He didn't care enough to check.

"You've quit your job for this?" He pressed, shaking his head. Delphine had a lot to answer for.

She nodded once. "My boss wouldn't allow me to have a sideline business. He said Singles Fest would directly compete with the hotel by hosting events. I had no choice but to leave. The more my plans came together, the more committed I became." She looked frustrated.

"Did you sign a non-compete?" Maybe Delphine hadn't suggested she leave her job. Then again, she knew people at the top over at the Sands. Someone or something drew her back here on a regular basis. He wouldn't put it past her to put the idea of discouraging Farren into her boss's head.

"A what?"

He sighed and realized he'd need to slow down.

"When you were hired," he said in a reasoning tone, "did you agree that if you left you wouldn't compete for their business?"

She frowned, but this was important, and she shouldn't need her hand held, not if this would be her new career. Going into business for yourself was not for the weak-kneed.

"No, I didn't sign anything like that." She waved both hands. "Besides, there's little chance of competing. I'm after a different demographic. Most single parents can't afford a place like the Sands. Not everyone who's divorced or widowed and raising children is a doctor or lawyer or stockbroker." She snorted. "Those people don't have any problem finding second wives and husbands and they can afford the Sands."

He detected a slightly bitter undertone to her last comment. He set that aside as too personal. He didn't care anyway.

"To be clear, you want to make a living from broke people. That's an interesting demographic."

Her brows knit and she looked confused by the question. He reacted to the way she nibbled her full lower lip in consternation.

"Well, when you put it that way—sure, it sounds less than ideal—but I'll go for quantity."

"Bargain basement matchmaking," he said with a note of wonder. She believed this would work. No one could be this naïve.

"Sort of. But not that." She looked so sure of herself, so committed, it took his breath. "When you make a decent living wage but have children, the money needs to go further and can't stretch to dates or meeting for a glass of wine or going to the movies and using a babysitter." She glared at him as if her troubles explaining herself were his fault.

He rubbed his chin and felt the lack of a shave. How long had it been, anyway? He scrubbed the scruff. A haircut and a shave were overdue.

"I must look like a bear," he muttered as the hole in his sock seemed to grow bigger as the seconds ticked by.

Startled, she giggled. The sound was crystalline and chiming. He almost smiled back at her.

"Yes, a bear. That's exactly right. But not a sleek black bear, more like a brown one. You know the ones you see in nature shows rubbing their backs on trees?"

He stared at her, but she was still lost in her imaginings of him in the woods. Her eyes shone with humor and her pouty soft lips curled up at the ends.

"Fine, I'll do something about it," he grumbled. She'd just compared him to a grizzly. At least the bear had an excuse.

She shrugged her beautiful, smooth shoulders. "No skin off my nose if you want to look like an old coot."

Old coot? Now she was being deliberately rude.

"I'm thirty-four."

"Big deal. Old is in your attitude, not the number of years you've lived."

"Now, who sounds like a senior citizen?" he prodded. "Would I be welcome at Singles Fest? I'm recently single again."

He hadn't thought of his situation in these terms before, but it was true. And he needed to get a handle on the market she was targeting. She seemed mixed up about where the profit would come from.

She shook her head no, which proved how confused she was. "Your situation is different. You were dealt a terrible blow, and everyone needs to grieve. But, given time, you'll find someone. When you're ready you'll have loads of women falling at your feet. You're Grady O'Hara and infinitely eligible."

"You called me an old coot and disparaged my attitude, not to mention the bear in the woods comparison and you think women will find me attractive?" This was fun. And somewhere Delphine was laughing. He'd call her when this was over. Despite cutting her out of his life, he wanted to rub her face in this mess.

"You're rich and single. With no children. Unless you've got some hidden away?"

At his head shake, she went on.

"Also, you've shown yourself willing to commit to marriage. Any woman in the market for a man would want you. Despite your supreme grumpiness. Besides, you don't have children, so technically you wouldn't fit in with what I have in mind."

He wanted to growl like the bear he supposedly was.

"You can't make a living on single parents alone. You'll need to expand to other markets. Your boss at the hotel knew that you'd come to that conclusion, given time." If she knew he was rich and single and showed no interest in him other than what his motel could bring to her business, then he could let her talk. And if thirty-four was an old coot, then how young was she?

Farren looked to be near his own age, but he was a poor judge of women's ages. Veronica had seemed young and carefree when they'd met. She'd been willing to travel the world at a moment's notice as his assistant, never complaining about the lack of personal time.

He knew why that was now. Hindsight and all that. He closed the door on the memories of how easily he'd been taken in. She'd been efficient, kind, and caring. The other employees sang her praises and Delphine had taken to her. Of course, she had because Delphine had hired her.

He snorted and Farren jumped at the sound. An idea formed but before the kernel could sprout, he crushed it. *No.*

Still, what if?

It would certainly get Delphine out of his hair. Maybe she'd give up on her relentless pursuit of a wife for him. You'd think she'd have learned the same way he had, but no. Here she was, sending this hapless woman to him.

A woman who likely needed a lot of guidance to get this idea off the ground. Or, conversely, needed to be scared off her plan.

Either way, he was the one to help her.

"I have a proposition for you," he said with the same smile he'd tried earlier. But this time, she didn't startle so easily. *Good.* She must be getting used to him.

"You're going to help me? Because the Fourth of July is right around the corner."

Clearly, he'd missed some salient points, but whatever. "Sure, I'll help. But first, I have a condition."

She looked wary but interested.

"I hate Delphine butting into my life. For lots of reasons, I want her to back off. I need you to pretend we've hit it off."

"In what way, exactly?" She leaned forward, avid. Farren Parks had no poker face. None at all. He had her and he knew it. This time when he smiled, she didn't flinch.

"Romantically."

"You want me to what?" Shock drained her face of color, but this was not the time to pity the woman.

"Tell my sister you got in here and I turned on the charm and now, we're dating. Tell her I'm helping you with Singles Fest. In return, you can do whatever you want with The Landseer. Fill it with parents and children if you want. Bring in a swinging singles club if that works. But you have to spend the summer here and pretend that we've got something going on."

Her face had now turned blood red and her neck looked ready to explode.

"Need a pat on the back?" he offered. That might help this all go down easier.

Chapter Four

"THAT MAKES NO SENSE," Farren sputtered after the shock wore off. Grady wanted to pretend they were dating. "Delphine won't believe it." Not after what she'd said about her brother being in deep grief.

He'd been hiding from the world. Everyone knew it. His fiancée had died, and he'd disappeared. Delphine was supposed to believe that one look at Farren would rock his world? She wanted to snort. Her brothers would howl if they heard.

"Her ego is so huge she'll believe it," Grady said. "Trust me on this."

Farren didn't know what to think but she couldn't fall in with his plan without knowing more, without pressing for details. Without being guaranteed the Landseer.

"Is this sexual harassment?" The question popped out uninvited. Of course, he wasn't interested in her in that way.

"You're not an employee of mine. And did I ask for any sexual favors?"

"Dating implies—"

"It's not like that." He shook his head. "No offense, but you're a little too sweet for me. Not my type at all." His gaze tracked her from her feet to the top of her head. No spark appeared in his eyes. She shouldn't feel deflated, but this was no surprise. She wasn't tall and willowy. He'd had his pick of New York models and gorgeous heiresses. Before his engagement, she'd seen pictures of him at The Met and movie premiers with high profile women. His fiancée had been lovely and statuesque, but a nobody before Grady.

No, Farren wasn't his type. The opposite in fact. Relief blended with a strange disappointment, but she set both aside to stay on track.

"I see. I'm too sweet. Of course. Nothing I haven't heard before." She should be relieved instead of vaguely insulted. He had no idea if she were sweet or not. She could be wildly inappropriate at times. Sort of. She'd had two glasses of wine with Delphine and spilled her guts, hadn't she? And she'd come here for three days just to push for something she wanted.

"You're no prize yourself," she tossed at him. Shaggy, unkempt, and with the personality of an alligator, Grady O'Hara was not her kind of man. He wore socks with holes in them and a shirt that had lost half the buttons.

"You won't have to do more than hold my hand occasionally, maybe let me throw my arm across your shoulders." He raised his hands palms out. "And that's only if Delphine's around. I haven't seen her in months, though, so those occasions would be rare."

"She's been staying at the Sands for a couple of weeks."

He shrugged. "Funny that she hasn't stopped by."

"Funny that you haven't invited her," she pressed. Another thought struck. "If we're dating, we'll have to be seen in public together. Not only for Delphine's sake."

"We'll go for lunch or dinner occasionally. The J Roger's still around, right? We could walk the beach if you want." He sighed as if the idea of being outside with her would be an ordeal. "We won't have to do much to get gossip started." He firmed his lips and gave a brisk nod.

Last Chance Beach kept gossip rolling, even when there wasn't much to say. She cast around for more benefits for herself. She needed more from him because he was asking a lot of her. While she was busy pretending for months that they were dating, she had to behave as if she was involved with him. Which meant if anyone interesting came along, she couldn't pursue a relationship.

She wasn't a cheater, not even if the relationship was fake. "If I agree to this *cockamamie*"—she scored a point with the jab— "plan of yours, then it's taking time away from my social life. I'm thirty-four, too and I can't date anyone else while I'm tied to you."

"Likewise for me," he pointed out. "But thirty-four is hardly ancient."

"It is if you're a woman who wants what I want."

He nodded. "Gotcha. The clock's ticking."

"Yes. Frankly, it is. I'd like to meet someone great and have a family with him."

"You'll still have time when we're done." He glared at her, insistent.

She moved on with a nod. "I need to see more people about my plan," she said consideringly. "You could come along some days." Scrap that. "No, what I mean to say is: I'll *need* you to come with me. You're not the only person who's been reluctant to see the benefits of my idea. And you did say Delphine should think you're helping me."

Barnacle Bill's Minigolf didn't want to offer group discounts in high season.

"The summer is when most of the businesses make their profit. I believe I can make Singles Fest popular at other times of the year, too, but for now, it'll be summer."

"Starting with the Fourth. Which is coming up fast," he repeated what she'd said earlier.

"Exactly. I'm running out of time. Wasting three days trying to get in to see you has been hard on my timeline." She was no pushover, and it was time he knew it.

"You'll want my support. You've got it." He nodded as if he were offering a blessing from on high. He could be quite full of himself. Another thing Delphine had said about him confirmed.

"When people learn you're behind me, it could make a difference." Some advantages came with his scheme, but tricking Delphine was the only reason he'd come up with the idea. "Do you think we can pull this off with your sister? Will she believe it?"

"Given what she put me through before, she'll jump at the idea that she's made things right for me."

According to online gossip he'd met his fiancée through work. And his sister was head of HR for his company. "Delphine found Veronica for you?"

"She convinced me to hire her as my assistant. Things went from there." He frowned and shifted in his seat. He snapped the footrest down and stood up, clearly in no mood to elaborate. Natural, given the terrible end of his fiancée. "Are we agreed?"

She nodded, although blaming his sister for Veronica's tragic drowning seemed off.

"Only until such time as my business is off the ground or for one year whichever comes first." There were some other stipulations she wanted, like him joining her for talks with reluctant venues. He agreed to everything. "I'd like a signed agreement if you don't mind. Simple language, please."

"Done. That's wise for both of us."

"I'll be a casual girlfriend. That's fine with me."

"Agreed."

"No more than occasional hugs and or kisses as warranted in a public place or in Delphine's presence."

"Great. I'm glad you see this the same way I do." He let his gaze rove over her from head to toe. "And you'll see no one else. No other dates. No other men."

"I'll give up a year of prime dating time for this. I expect you to do the same."

"Exclusive. Got it," he agreed.

There was no way around giving away a full year of her life in her mid-thirties. She hoped her sacrifice was worth it. A year at her age was more valuable than in her twenties. She wanted to raise children with a committed partner. Finding one might take time.

She stood and held out her hand to shake his. He clasped it and gave her one brisk shake. She didn't feel a thing but warm fingers clasping hers. No zip or zing or attraction. Good. Being attracted to Grady O'Hara would be a new level of hell.

"How soon do we start?" she asked.

"Tomorrow's fine. Come over in the morning and we'll do a walk through the motel to check things over."

She'd been in his presence for less than an hour and her whole life had been turned upside down. For the next year. Nerves fluttered in her low belly. This seemed simple enough, so why the nerves?

She had what she'd come for; access to the motel, his approval to include the motel in her promotion of Singles Fest, and, as a bonus, his advice on her business plan. She'd be a fool to pass all this up.

She had little to lose. Her job was already gone. Her acquaintanceship with Delphine could suffer, but they hadn't been real friends. And her pride could take the knock when this fake relationship came to an end next year. Meantime, though, it might prove helpful for clients to think that Singles Fest had already worked for her and Grady.

A long-term single matchmaker had terrible optics for her business. Appearing faithful in a fake relationship might become a burden if an interested man suddenly appeared in her life, but she didn't see that happening anytime soon.

Her nervous flutters settled, and she gave Grady a quick nod. "I'll do a walk around the exterior now, if you don't mind."

"Knock yourself out. You can report what you find tomorrow." With that, he shut the door, leaving her outside alone.

"Okay, thanks," she said to no one. She pulled out her phone to create a new file about the exterior of the building.

She dictated whatever she saw. The structure was as she remembered it. The motel contained thirty units, fifteen to a side. The house was attached to the backside of the left wing with a short narrow breezeway through to the center courtyard where the pool and playground were. Grady would have his privacy.

The motel office sat facing the center court and, in the distance, the ocean. The U-shape of the property made it perfect for families. Children could play in the pool within view of the motel room windows and the playground sat beside the pool, closer to the ocean. The fenced pool and play equipment were separated by a gate. Chain link meant children in both enclosures could be seen. Wooden benches ringed the pool fence and wooden loungers sat in groups of two, four and six. She assumed the pads were stored in the pool supply shed next to the office.

"I hope the lounge pads have been replaced since I worked here," she said into her phone. "Check for that in the morning."

If Grady did as he said and walked with her as they went from room to room in the morning, she'd have to speak clearly and include his comments when he spoke. She couldn't afford to miss anything they talked about.

She wandered down the left side units and found the ancient ice machine. "Get Grady to replace this old thing with a larger unit." The vending machines were long gone. "Call a vending company to come out."

After that, the walk around went smoothly, and she felt validated about choosing The Landseer for her first hosting property. She'd want others, of course, but they would come with time. She had her eye on a B&B, but she wasn't sure if Sandpiper Cottage could accommodate children comfortably.

An hour later, back at home, she gathered her thoughts and her nerve and called Delphine to report on her meeting with Grady. The other woman had sent multiple texts asking how things were going. She knew that it had taken three days to get an audience with the big, shaggy grump, so she was antsy.

Delphine answered immediately. "Well, how was my brother? Accommodating?"

"Yes, after I talked my way inside. After that, he turned charming." Farren felt heat rise in her cheeks at the lie. Good thing they weren't on a video chat. Farren was a blushing liar. It was the only time she blushed, being raised with three rambunctious brothers had inured her to the ridiculous interest boys had in bodily functions and keeping score. And protecting their little sister from other rambunctious boys.

Her high school years had been a nightmare. Until Denny Bracken in her senior year. For some reason, her brothers had approved of him. Maybe they'd known that his feelings for her were all surface and therefore no threat. Or maybe by then they were too involved in their own lives to keep watch over hers. College and new careers had overtaken her brothers and she'd finally been free of their oversight.

She wondered what they'd think of Grady O'Hara's lack of grooming. His hair hadn't been cut in far too long, his clothes looked way past comfortably broken in and his socks had been unraveling before her eyes.

Funny, once you see a hole in a sock, you can't unsee it. She wondered if he'd toss the pair away. Maybe not.

"How did he look?" Delphine asked in Farren's ear. She set the phone on her small desk and turned on the speaker.

"Fine. A bit shaggy, but he looked happy"—yes, his sister would want to hear that— "and well-fed. He'd grilled himself a steak." That much was true, she'd smelled the barbecue when she'd climbed out of her car. Her mouth had watered, reminding her that she'd had a light supper. She opened her fridge to check the contents. Great, she had the makings for a salad.

She pulled out greens and radishes and leftover chicken to shred for the top. Giving the fridge door a hip shot to close it, she set the food on the counter. "He's fine," she repeated when Delphine went silent.

"I see." Delphine drawled. "And how was he charming? What did he say that was so charming?"

It was an odd question even for a nosy sister, which Farren now believed. Grady was right about Delphine's matchmaking. The thought made her belly flutter. "He smiled a lot and joked. And he's friendly. I don't know why you say he's grouchy. He was happy to see me." She rolled her eyes at the blatant lie.

"Really?" Delphine sounded doubtful, but Farren chose silence instead of reassurance. She might blush when lying but she knew babbling was a mistake. Lying to her brothers had made her an expert at silent lies of omission.

After a moment, Delphine broke the silence, apparently convinced. "Good. Then you hit it off?"

Farren shifted. "In a manner of speaking. We're seeing each other in the morning, and he suggested lunch, too." They'd have to be seen in public together for the gossip mill to begin its inexorable grind toward announcing their couple status. Once the gossip reached Delphine, she'd believe the charade. "I hope you don't mind. I know he's been through a lot, but a friendly lunch is harmless."

"Just don't break his heart and we'll be good."

There was no concern on that front. Farren was not a heartbreaker. More the heartbreakee. "How long are you in town?"

"I can manage a few more days," Delphine replied. "Then it's back to the grind."

Surely Delphine would believe they were a couple by then. Farren could stop lying about finding the big brown bear of a man attractive. She made a mental note to let him know they had a lunch 'date.'

Chapter Five

6:45 A.M.

Grady grunted as he read his phone. Lunch with Farren. *Huh.* She'd sent the text last night, but he'd been asleep, and he never slept with his phone within earshot. It was a habit that Veronica had instilled. She'd insisted that a decent night's sleep would be better than hearing about unsolvable problems at one a.m. And since his business was international, calls had indeed, come in during the wee hours.

Once he'd instituted the change, his staff had learned that whatever they had to say could wait. Clients were another matter, but they had learned to check the timing of their calls. They'd all gone to voicemail after eleven p.m.

He scrubbed his head and stared into the bathroom mirror over the sink. His fingers rolled over his jaw, scrubbing at the thick scruff. Tilting his head up he tracked the coarse hair down his neck.

Had he planned to have lunch with Farren? No, he'd remember if he had. She'd left his house after they'd made their deal. She'd planned to walk around the exterior of the motel and make notes. This morning, they planned to check out the interiors of the units and then…nothing. He hadn't set a time for the walk-through either. And he hadn't invited her to lunch.

He'd been in a hurry to get Farren out of his home and off his mind. He'd succeeded with one but not the other. Little Farren Parks had stuck in his head all night. Her earnest belief in this crazy idea made him curious. Even when he'd pointed out the flaws in her plan, she hadn't blinked.

Surely, she realized how little profit there'd be catering to people with limited discretionary income. Maybe she'd slept on it and realized he was right. But the determined glint in her eye last night made him doubt she had second thoughts.

He texted back. "Be here at ten. Then we'll walk the beach to the J Roger."

Farren didn't respond, but he knew she'd be on time. She was too well organized not to show up. This was a big day for her.

He ignored the cryptic text he had from Delphine asking him what he thought about Singles Fest. Let her stew. She'd fall over dead if he answered her anyway. Even if he couldn't bear to talk with her, he'd notice if his sister fell over dead. He shrugged. Delphine could wait. She'd made her move by sending Farren to him. Now, she'd have to be patient.

Besides, he was sure Farren had spilled her guts to Delphine the moment she could. Yes. From the length of his hair to the holes in his socks, Farren would've talked.

By ten o'clock he'd run his errands and returned home. He pulled into one of his two parking spots in front of his small veranda on the back side of the motel. From the front of the motel, his home entrance couldn't be seen. He liked it. He just drove around back, and the place was all his.

Over the veranda was a balcony with a view to die for. Looking north, from up there he saw no signs of habitation except for the occasional rooftop with a satellite dish. And sand dunes and miles of beach and ocean.

A bright orange electric car sat neat as a pin in one of his two spots. The owner, likely Farren, was nowhere to be seen.

He climbed out of his rental SUV and headed toward his front door. As he rounded the hood of the vehicle, he saw Farren on his lone plastic chair in the shade of the veranda. She had her eyes on her laptop screen until he stood right in front of her. It wasn't until he cleared his throat that she looked up, startled.

Dressed as she was in cut-off shorts that hit mid-thigh and a white cotton blouse with the tail tied over her waist, she looked full Island Girl. Pretty, casual, and ready for anything beachy.

He'd planned to stroll the beach on the way to lunch. He hadn't walked the beach much since arriving. The breeze should clear his head, the salt air would invigorate him, and the company would be...stimulating.

Gulls screeched overhead. No surprise. It was garbage pickup day. The sky scroungers paid attention and knew the schedule.

"Hello," she said in a bright, interested tone. She closed her tablet and smiled, holding out her hand to shake. "I'm Farren Parks." He ignored her offered hand.

"Very funny." He pulled out his key and unlocked his door. He pushed inside and held the door open for her.

Farren remained outside, mouth gaping. "You shaved and got a haircut." Her gaze ran over his body looking for other changes.

"Threw out all my old socks, too," he quipped as he held up a department store bag that contained new socks and underwear. Not that she'd see the underwear, but once he'd taken a good look at what he was wearing under his jeans—well—he wasn't an animal despite what she thought.

"I'll put this stuff away and be right with you. There could be a cup of old coffee left in the machine. Help yourself."

"No, I'm good," she said faintly.

He caught sight of himself in the hall mirror on the way to his bedroom. He stopped and turned back. She still stood framed in the doorway. "You didn't recognize me, did you?"

Farren shook her head. "I assumed you were a brother or maybe a cousin?" She framed it as a question, but it proved her confusion at his appearance.

He hadn't realized how low he'd sunk before he'd stepped into the barber shop. The barber, fresh out of barber college, had accepted the challenge with relish. He'd asked to take before and after pictures, but Grady had refused.

No way did he want his before photos sold to a gossip rag.

He left Farren, still looking surprised by the changes, and tossed his booty on top of his unmade bed. It was time he gave a damn again. He would change the sheets later and put out fresh towels in the bathroom. Maybe he'd run a load of laundry. Feeling brighter than he had in weeks, Grady returned to his guest as she waited by the main door to the house.

He crowded her so he could close the door at her back.

"Let's get moving, I've got a lot to do today," he snapped. She smelled great. Something light and spicy. He breathed deeply to enjoy her scent. "Go through the kitchen door, it's closer to the motel office."

She started at the sound of his deep inhale. Her gaze cut to his as she moved off.

"Right," she murmured and strode quickly through the house. Almost as if he frightened her.

It was just a sniff. Not as if he breathed fire. Clearly, he'd been alone too long if he'd begun sniffing women. He gave a mental shrug.

"Look," he explained, "I had to clean up or Delphine would never believe we're dating."

"Okay. That makes sense. And, basically, that's why I tacked on lunch today. I told her that when we met last night you made jokes and promised this walk-through and invited me to lunch." She exited the kitchen door, giving him room to pass. Her scent, oddly enticing now, drifted by again, but he controlled his urge to lean in for more. He'd already scared her once.

"I should have checked with you first about lunch," she continued apologetically, "but when Delphine and I talked, it seemed natural that since I was claiming you and I hit it off and you'd been charming, that we'd go for lunch." She pursed her lips. "I asked if she minded if we saw each other socially. I called it a friendly lunch."

He chuckled. "You told her I was charming?" That was a new way to describe the reception he'd given her. "She must have wondered about that." He hadn't been charming since Veronica had been his assistant for six months. And then, it was more Veronica laying on the charm.

Looking back, he couldn't pinpoint a time when he'd decided to make a play for Veronica. He'd gotten into the habit of laughing with her because Veronica had been funny. She'd had a great sense of humor and he'd fallen for it. She'd also been smart and efficient. Of course, he'd notice, which was what Delphine had counted on.

"I wouldn't know what Delphine wondered about. I let the lie hang in the air until she accepted it."

His chuckle turned into a full out laugh and she looked startled by the sound. He admitted it sounded like rust on hinges.

"You've got a pair of steels, there." The next time she let a comment hang, he'd know what she was doing. Farren Parks was a strategist. His chest warmed.

"No, not steel balls." She shook her head and smiled widely, her plump lower lip stretched and shiny. "What I do have are older brothers and if I wanted to get away with anything in Last Chance Beach, I had to learn how to be convincing. And babbling through a lie is a sure way to get caught."

"Silence works." He nodded, intrigued, and pleased. Now who was laying on the charm?

"Most of the time, yes," she said with a sly grin. "Especially on a call. Once I was old enough to have my own cell phone, my life got a lot easier." The mischief in her gaze caught him and he got a glimpse of the cheeky teenager she'd once been. Her hair had been tamed with a clip at the nape of her neck, but shorter wisps had escaped to dance around her face.

"What would a sweet girl like you have to lie about in this small town? I can't see you running with a street gang or looking for wild thrills with the local bad boy."

"See? You can be charming and funny," she quipped.

He raised his index finger skyward. "I know," he exclaimed. "You were sneaking off to the local lovers' lane."

She blushed. "Eventually. After my last brother left for college."

He laughed again. This time he sounded more natural, less rusty. "You must know every nook and cranny of the island."

She nodded. "I plan to share the most romantic and private places with my couples." She cleared her throat. "Only if they reach a point in their relationship where romance and privacy come into play."

"You've given these plans of yours more thought than I expected. You want to be hands-on with your matches?" She'd considered so much more than numbers and profit versus expenses. And this was more service than a dating app offered.

"I want to give them the chance to let their feelings bloom. Maybe those feelings will take root."

"You don't think that's intrusive." His voice came out harsher than he meant. But this sounded so much like what had happened to him. *Gentle persuasion. Manipulation. Betrayal of trust.*

She straightened at his tone. "Sometimes nature taking its course takes too long and most people, especially the second time around, need a prod." She sighed and moved away, tossing back another comment over her shoulder. "I want to set the mood when people are clearly interested in each other. That's all."

"And you're an expert on what couples need to connect? And on second chances?"

He caught up to her and saw her blanch. "Not exactly. But their time here will be short, and they'll need to make the most of it. There's nothing wrong with offering an unexpected bonus of a private, romantic spot."

WHAT HAD JUST HAPPENED? Grady had almost made her admit her lack of a love life. Not only had she not grabbed for a second chance at love, but she also barely recalled her first chance. Sure, she'd dated since returning home from college, but the men who'd asked her out had been tourists and looking for an easy, casual holiday fling. Some had only been looking for one-night stands and they held no appeal for Farren.

So, she'd dated sporadically for a week here and there. When the local available men she knew left town none of them had come back. And the one she'd have left for didn't ask. Denny Bracken had left for college without inviting her and she'd let him go without a fight.

No biggie now, of course, because she'd moved on into her career. Until lately, she'd been content enough. But feeling the fire of ambition around Singles Fest had lit another fire, too. As Grady had so succinctly put it, at thirty-four her clock was ticking.

When the news had broken a couple of months ago that Denny Bracken had two families simultaneously in adjoining states she'd been floored. Here she was, wanting one family of her own and he had two. Technically it wasn't bigamy, but that's what the locals were calling it.

She had to agree. Neither family knew of the other and since he was splitting his time between them, that looked a lot like bigamy.

Farren preferred her men not to have second wives and families one state over.

The Denny she remembered had been fun and handsome. He'd always been sweet to her and in his own way, honest. He'd never made any promises and if she'd had hopes for a future with him, that was on her. Girls had liked him. They'd come easily to him and for a time, she'd been one of them. High school drama, all of it.

Still, Denny leaving her behind had been the start of a trend she'd soured on.

As she walked by Grady, she wondered if he'd smell her hair again. He didn't, but she took a sniff of him. He smelled of aftershave and clean man. Very pleasant. Up close this way she could tell he'd shaved closely. His jaw looked smooth and clean and the skin soft as butter.

Once inside the standard-looking motel room, she spoke. "This one shouldn't take long to clean and air out." She studied the newish mattresses on the two queen beds. They didn't sag or otherwise look worn. The mini-fridge, small microwave, and counter looked relatively new and clean.

"Check out the bathroom," Grady said in a dire tone.

She walked past the beds and turned to look through the bathroom door.

"Oh, I see." The tile had seen better days in the bath/shower combination. Dead bugs littered the bottom of the tub. Flies, mostly. "The drywall looks fine, though. No mold. No water stains."

"True," he said from close behind her. She shifted but there was nowhere to go to get away from how great he smelled. "One of those bathroom sheathing companies could cover the tile walls and tub. That would refresh it quickly."

His breath stirred the hair near her temple. She should have scraped it back into a tight bun or put the clip higher, so no strands escaped. Next time, she'd have her hair under tight control. He was clearly into sniffing. And the feel of him so close at her back sent tingles to places where she shouldn't tingle. Not with him. Not for him.

And definitely not when they were faking it.

"The counter looks new enough." On the end near the toilet a single brown spot marred the surface where someone had left a burning cigarette. "So much for being a smoke-free room." Looking down, she toed the linoleum. "And the floor's been replaced."

"Okay, good," he said and scooched past her. Their shoulders brushed as he opened the small window over the toilet. "This is sticky, but an easy fix." The close quarters were playing havoc with her good sense. She pulled her mind back to the job at hand.

Fresh ocean air filled the small space when he opened the window. "We can hear the surf. That's great. Very soothing."

Her spirits rose as she took it all in. "The tub and shower will take the longest to do and it's a fast process. Maybe they could do them all in a couple of days if we find more like this."

"We need to check the linens, to see how threadbare they are." Grady added with a considering tone. He backed out of the bathroom, giving her room to breathe again.

"Nice towels are important. But this will be a budget conscious place, so medium thick would be fine," she said. "I'd have thought you'd have checked the linen supply already."

His eyes glowed with humor as he shook his head. "I had no plans to open the motel, remember? This is all for you." He crossed his arms over his expansive chest. In his plaid shirt he looked amazingly like a lumberjack on a package of paper towels. She blinked and he looked like Grady again. Heaven help her if she ever saw him in a toolbelt.

"It isn't all for me," she insisted. "By helping me, you'll get Delphine off your back."

He shrugged.

"So why live here? Why not sell the motel right away?" Last Chance Beach was a rough-cut jewel in the midst of a good polish. The Landseer would be an easy sale, especially for an international real estate broker.

Grady frowned and his voice went husky. "Maybe what I was doing wasn't really living."

"Oh," she said because she couldn't think of one other single thing to say.

Grady had shaved and got a haircut and *she hadn't recognized him. At all.*

Worse yet, he knew it. How embarrassing for him. One clean up and he was a new man. A handsome man. He had a strong jaw and perfect teeth except for the slightly turned one next to his front two. She liked that small difference, it made him seem more real somehow.

Too bad his personality couldn't have an easy makeover.

He was still a grump and that was what she should focus on. His light auburn hair and gorgeous blue eyes could be seen now. Last night Grady had been a bushman who'd looked miserable and unwelcoming and like the last person on earth who'd make a good hotelier.

The barber had done a great job styling the mop that had been on his head. Smooth sides with a nice healthy top that showed waves, not a tangled mess.

Unfortunately, she liked how he looked. She frowned at him.

"If I agree to open this place fully, then I'll need to hire staff." He frowned. "I didn't want to be bothered with people asking questions and getting in my face."

"You've already agreed," she pointed out. She understood. Staff was expensive and the ones from before had been laid off when his great-aunt had passed away. "I could ask around to see if any of the previous staff are available."

"You'll need a manager, a couple of desk clerks, and housekeeping covered," he stated firmly. "I won't interact with the guests in any way. My house is private and off-limits and that needs to be made clear. I don't want to hear any kids screaming or parents yelling at them."

He may be cleaned up, but he was still a grouch. Still unapproachable. And what was his thing about hating families?

"This unit is too close to my house. You can't use it for guests."

"But that's—"

He held up a hand, cutting her off. "Don't care. I won't have anyone sharing the breezeway who'll have the tv blaring and kids bouncing off the walls."

Technically the guests wouldn't use the breezeway because the door to this unit faced the courtyard. He was being difficult for no reason other than to exert his authority. Fine. She'd find another use for this space.

"Okay. But what about the bathroom? Should we bother getting this room ready?"

"We'll get it done. Might as well if the crew is here anyway."

At least she'd got something out of him. She nodded her acceptance as they made their way into the unit next door. This one was in better shape. Slightly. The bathroom had no cigarette burns anywhere.

After that, the notes became easier, and the conversation relegated to the simplest comments.

By the time they'd reached the last unit, Grady was frowning.

"If this place is full, I'll hear a lot of noise at my place. Maybe I'll move out for the high season."

"But what about us hanging out together?" she blurted. "Delphine will wonder."

"We'll cross that bridge later," he said with another frown. He patted his stomach. "I'm ready for lunch. You?"

"Lead on."

They strolled down to the beach on a grey, weathered, wooden walkway that had seen better days. "I'll replace these loose boards."

"I can bring someone in."

"No need. I've done some carpentry. I can cut wood and hammer nails. Besides, it'll be good to get out into the fresh air."

"You're full of surprises," she said. "I thought you wanted to be hands off."

"Fixing boards is different. I can do it alone."

They turned as one to see the motel from the beach. It sat, white and clean, with a bright blue roof that matched the blue of the pool. His house's second story was the tallest point. From here, she could see a balcony over the veranda. "You must have a great view from the second floor."

"I do. The balcony is off the bedroom. Nice to sit out there and have a coffee first thing."

"That's why you don't want people next door to you. They would disturb your morning coffee."

"The way the house sits I see nothing but dunes and grasses. And the whitecaps, of course. My slice of heaven. But sound travels and why ruin a good view with screaming brats?"

Ignoring his comment, she turned to continue the stroll to the water's edge. Other people were holding hands and walking as the waves lapped at their feet. A jogger joined another as they headed south. The breeze lifted her hair, and she felt the cotton of her blouse press against her skin. "I love the beach."

"Me, too." His voice was thoughtful. "I haven't been out here in too long."

"Then welcome back."

"Thanks."

They strolled in companionable silence for twenty minutes before she spoke again.

"I've been thinking about that first unit," she said. "What if I moved in there? Without a job and all I have going into the business, living at the motel makes sense. You clearly don't need the income from the unit, or you'd be willing to fill it."

"You're asking to live rent free?" He looked at the sky as he replied.

"Only until this fake relationship is over and the business has taken off." She wasn't asking to live there forever, just for the high season. "With the launch being the Fourth, I'll be at the motel all day long all summer long anyway."

He laughed and the rusty sound of it grated across her ears, but she smiled in response. "You drive a hard bargain, Farren. I like that."

"I promise to be quiet and not disturb you."

He cast her a sidelong glance. "Even if I had a 'Do Not Disturb' sign on my forehead, you'd disturb me. Who's the one who came back for three days straight, peering through windows and banging on my door?"

"Me, that would be me," she admitted. "And I'll pay rent if you need me to."

He shook his head and rolled his shoulders. "You're something."

"What? You don't want me there to handle the families if they need something?"

"Yes, I do. The unit's yours, along with all the responsibility for your guests."

Chapter Six

AT THE J ROGER, GRADY held Farren's seat for her and then took the one opposite. The tabletop sat on an old oak barrel, and he had to spread his knees wide to get comfortable. The server, a harried young woman with her hair held up in a bun that sat square on top of her head, approached briskly, and asked for their drinks order. Grady waited for the swaying bundle of hair to topple into her face, but gravity failed him.

No one came to The J Roger expecting fancy service. Nothing had changed since he'd tried using a fake ID at nineteen. Remembering his manners, he looked at a happy Farren. "The lady will have?" he asked her.

"A beer's fine," she said with a small grin for the server.

"Two beers. We'll let you know our food order when you get back." The lunch crowd was arriving. "We were lucky to get a table. This place is busier than I recall."

"We're the early crowd. After this, the next group, mostly tourists, will hang out taking in the view. Locals want to eat and run." The breeze picked up a couple of loose tendrils of her hair, some catching on her plump lower lip. She slid her tablet to the tabletop and opened it. "I need to check that we've seen and discussed all we need to this morning."

"Don't get too involved or this won't look like a date." He exaggerated a cloak and dagger scan of the busy restaurant. There was indoor seating, but the day was perfect, with a cloudless sky and a soft ocean breeze. It had been a no-brainer to choose to sit in the open air.

She flushed a light pink at his silly reminder of their farce. A wayward tendril of hair caught on her lip, and he fought the urge to reach over and remove it to fly free again. She got it herself in an absent gesture.

"You're right. I should close this. I'm sure we covered everything." She shoved her tablet into her bag and leaned toward him, pretending to look interested. As she leaned in, he could just make out the line of shadow between her breasts. She was fulsome, and sweetly seductive in her innocent appearance. Beneath her blouse was a hot pink tank top that clung like a second skin. Her shorts moved higher on her thighs, and he forced his gaze to drop. Like most locals, she wore flip flops on her feet. Her toenails were painted a rosy pink. Subtle, and pretty all over, Farren made him smile despite his apparent grouchiness.

He hoped she didn't think he looked like a bear anymore.

They'd strolled a good length of beach to get here, mostly in silence. He'd enjoyed the walk, the sunshine, and the peace they seemed to both enjoy. Farren could be a talker when she needed, but she also recognized the value in companionable quiet.

No seductress here, not in the way Veronica had been. But then, she'd been subtle in the beginning, too. Once Grady had shown interest, Veronica's approach had moved friendly to seductive. He quickly looked up and away before Farren caught him leering down her tank top like a teenager. The Rock, a boulder the size of a small house, stood sentinel over the beach, covered in lovers' graffiti. He was happy to see the tradition continued.

"Farren, are you here for lunch?" A happy, female voice came closer with each word.

"Hi, Eva. Yes, I'm here with Grady," she responded with a small wave for the new arrival and a slight nod in his direction.

Not to be dissuaded, Eva walked up to their table for two. She shoved her hand toward Grady. "Nice to meet you, Grady." The tall blonde gave him the once over, her eyes bright and happy.

Grady gave her a salute and then took her hand for a perfunctory shake. "Hello, Eva. You're friends with Farren?"

"Have been since I moved here six months ago. She's the best." Eva waggled her eyebrows and included Farren. "Are you the owner of the Landseer?" she probed, obviously aware of Farren's interest in talking to him.

"I am," he said gravely.

Farren tilted her head, amused. He had no idea what brought on her look, but at least she wasn't scowling.

"Eva is a daycare operator," Farren explained, though he hadn't asked. "Or she will be when she opens later this year. For the summer she's helping me with Singles Fest. I'll have to offer daycare or early evening care for date nights and adult time."

"That's where I come in," Eva added.

"Right." Surprised at Farren's forethought, he smiled and gave both women a nod. "I'm not a father so kids and their needs don't impact me. But it seems you've thought of everything." Impressed with Farren's thoroughness, he wondered where a weak spot would appear in her plan. Because there was always at least one.

"I'm trying," Farren responded. "Note to self: find babysitters for infants."

"Farren keeps lists," Eva said with a grin. "Lots and lots of lists."

"I must or I won't keep it all straight. There's a lot to juggle."

He imagined there would be. She was trying to anticipate the needs of several families at once, with every child's age group covered. "Kids need different activities at different ages. How will you provide for everyone?"

"Lists," she responded. "Lots and lots of lists." She chuckled. "Now you know why I need them."

"And she has me to advise her on that," Eva added.

"Send me your lists," he said. "I'll take a look." He'd probably been wrong to ask her to put away her tablet.

"Eva! Your order's up." A voice from the take-out counter bawled.

"Fish and chips, my favorite from here," Eva said. "So long for now. Farren, call me later, okay?"

"Okay," she promised with a roll of her eyes. She went pink in the cheeks as if there were a hidden female message in the simple request.

As Eva picked her way through the tables away from them, Grady pounced. "Why the eye-roll?"

"She assumes we're here on a date." She lifted one smooth shoulder and dropped it.

"That's a good thing. It's what we want."

She brightened. "That's right. It's exactly what we want. Except Eva doesn't gossip."

"When you talk to her later, confirm that we're seeing each other." He reconsidered. "Or, that lunch was more than work. That might be the better way to go."

"So, you're giving me lessons in fake dating now?"

"Fake me, baby," he blurted, to get a laugh.

The server set their frosted glasses of beer on the table and raised her eyebrows at his comment. He glared at her. "I said 'fake me,' not the word you think you heard."

Farren burst out laughing.

The server grinned. "Whatever. It's pretty clear what you meant." She pivoted and tossed Farren a saucy smile before stepping away.

"Now, *that*, will get us noticed," Farren said as her shoulders rolled through her full-throated bout of laughter. "Good job, Grady." She leaned low across the table toward him, deepening the shadow between her breasts. "For sure Delphine will hear about this. Fake me, baby. Too funny."

He frowned. It was the totally wrong impression for his sister. He wanted to show her that he'd woken from his recent stasis, not that he was ready to ravish unsuspecting innocents, like Farren.

He took a sip of beer to wet his dry throat and tried not to think about that other F word. "What's the story with Eva? She's been here six months?"

"Yes, she's a good friend and she's finally settled on a location for her daycare. She's calling it NanaBanana. One word. She thinks the name will appeal to the children. She's made up a song they'll sing."

"It seems to me there's a lot of entrepreneurial spirit in town. I don't recall businesses opening here when I used to come as a kid. A lot of storefronts were closed." Last Chance Beach had seemed to be on its last legs. "What happened?"

She shrugged. "A few years ago, the Sands opened and that brought us people who'd never heard of Last Chance Beach. Word spread about how unspoiled the beaches are, how quiet and relaxing it is. But new development followed once word of mouth kicked in and now, the town's in the throes of trying to hold onto the old peace and quiet while trying to benefit from more hustle."

"The land the Landseer sits on would be worth a fortune."

She shifted, looking uncomfortable. "It would, I guess, but if you sold it, my business would suffer."

He reached across the table and patted her hand where it rested beside her glass. "You don't need to worry. I'm not sure what I'll decide to do with the place. I like it just the way it is."

For now, he'd keep the motel. But later, no one knew what life would bring. He was the poster child for not seeing what was right in front of him. Blind, deaf, and gullible, Grady had learned the hard way that today was today, and no one was promised tomorrow.

He'd like to see how well Farren could do with this Singles Fest idea. Something about it appealed to him. Maybe it was the wacky optimism he saw glowing from Farren's eyes. Maybe it was that she had a mountain of details to conquer. Maybe it was the woman herself.

He wasn't sure she'd make a go of Singles Fest, but it would be fun to watch. And for now, fun was all he wanted. He smoothed his fingers across the back of her capable hand and decided it was fine place to rest his fingers.

And the gesture would make him look more interested in Farren than he was. To curious eyes only.

Because he wasn't interested. Not at all.

Chapter Seven

THERE WAS A LOT MORE Farren could say to Grady about Eva, but she preferred to keep her friend's secrets. Grady needn't know that Eva had abandoned a high-powered career and life in Los Angeles to come here and care for other people's children.

Eva Fontaine needed a simple life now. One filled with laughter and singing and fun. What's more, she deserved it. And her daycare would give her all the joy she needed. Singles Fest would fill her days until NanaBanana opened.

Grady's hand rested on hers comfortably and she enjoyed the sensation of heat and gentle caring. His eyes were warm, and she couldn't tell if it was manufactured for the curious or if he felt something real. Whatever. It was lovely to raise her face to the sun, feel the weight of his hand on hers and know that this man was on her side.

"Thanks for reassuring me about the motel," she said as she covered the hand that covered hers. She patted him contentedly. Three hands stacked like pancakes. A gull screeched overhead when another snatched up a fry a tourist had tossed to the sand.

"Locals never feed the gulls. They get grabby if you stop. Not to mention the dive bombing."

"I remember," he said with a chuckle. "They have remarkable aim."

She shouldn't feel closer to him for this innocent touch of hands, but she did. Anyone looking at them would believe they were interested in each other. The thought gave her pause. Where was the grumpy bear she'd come to know?

"Ready to order?" he asked. "Those fish and chips sound like a good idea."

"That's what I'll have, too. The chalkboard claims the fish slept in the sea last night. That's how fresh it is." They still sat with their hands stacked in the classic lovers' pose over the table. "This looks good," she offered and moved her hand a bit. "Like we mean it."

"Faking it seems easy enough. You still okay with it? I pressed you to agree." He frowned. "Let me know if anything I do is too much or pushes your boundaries."

"I will. I'm no pushover. We agreed light touching, hand-holding, affectionate kisses in front of your sister if the situation calls for them."

"Right. Like if we're taking our leave or greeting each other."

"Or you do something sweet for me. Like bring me a rose or do something extra-nice."

"Do I need to make lots and lots of lists?" he teased.

"Or say something funny, just to make me laugh," she added. Her heart did a pit-a-pat.

"Have I thanked you properly for agreeing to this charade? Delphine has been a pain in my, er, neck for too long. Mostly about women. She thinks I have the potential to be—"

"A very lonely man," she finished for him. "She's mentioned that a few times. It's out of concern, and since…" she trailed away, afraid to ruin this pleasant camaraderie.

"Since my fiancée drowned the night before the wedding, she's been worse. I think she's convinced I'll never find another Veronica."

Farren didn't know what to say to that. Clearly, he wanted the love of his life back.

He caught the server's attention and during the seconds it took for her to arrive at their table, they separated their hands. The moment of friendliness collapsed as they placed their orders.

When he looked back at her, he said, "I guess we should fill in time with small talk." He grimaced and she recognized the grouch who'd been missing a moment ago.

"I think you hate small talk."

"That obvious?" He unwrapped his cutlery from the paper napkin, but still looked at her with interest. What was he after? It wasn't chit-chat.

She sipped at her beer and waited.

"We should do the usual get-to-know-you stuff. Delphine may quiz you. Ask whatever you want," he said.

She gave a quick shake of her head. "You start. That way, I'll know when you get tired of the small talk. Or bored."

"I'll tell you when I've heard enough." Brusque, pointed. Grady. "You've got brothers. How many?"

"Three, all older."

"Live here?"

"No. But close enough that I see them regularly."

"Parents?"

"Live on the mainland. They wanted to be closer to the grandkids. And the airport for travel."

She could see boredom setting in behind his eyes. Before it took hold, she had questions of her own.

"My turn."

He nodded, looking wary. "Veronica is off limits."

"Understandable." No way did she want to discuss his fiancée. Too soon and too hard. But his sister cared about him, and it made her curious that he refused to see Delphine. But anyone could see Grady was still grieving. His sister should respect that, shouldn't she? So maybe Grady had it wrong and Farren wasn't the next eligible woman his sister had found for him. "Why does Delphine think you need help finding women?"

"Ask her. I've always been perfectly happy alone." He sighed. "My sister has butted into my life ever since we lost our mom when we were fourteen. I think she took on the role of mothering in her grief and hasn't figured out yet that she can let it go."

"You were busywork? And now, with Veronica's accident..." she trailed off because she'd put her foot in her mouth. Again.

"Busywork is a good word for it. Managing me kept her mind off her own loss when we were kids. That's why I allowed it for too long. And now it's shaping up to get worse."

They fell to silence while she pondered being fourteen and losing your mother. She shuddered inwardly. A moment later she blew out a breath.

"Okay. Before Veronica, were there any other women that were long-term?" Curiosity was a terrible thing sometimes. But figuring out what made some men loners and others hound dogs could be important. She had a list of questions for men's profiles, but Grady's answers might shed light where there was none before.

Her brothers were gregarious and friendly with women, but were they hound dogs? She hoped not, since two of them were married. She frowned.

Grady gave a shake of his head. "I was too busy for long term. A month or two, but nothing longer. Before Veronica, my women friends told me women want to spend time with the man they're dating."

"Go figure," she quipped.

He lifted a corner of his lip at her cheekiness. "Back then, I was busy building O'Hara and didn't hear them. I figured they stayed, or they didn't." He gave her an indifferent shrug.

"Women were conveniences?" *Wow, okay.*

He shifted. "I guess. But it wasn't deliberate." He dropped his gaze to the tabletop and frowned darkly. Her question must have hit a nerve. *Good.*

But she understood more about him now. Veronica had been building the business with him as his assistant. It made sense that a busy man would find a woman close at hand. Working late together, travelling together, sharing take-out at their desks as the city slowed to a night crawl. If they were both single, it would be natural to fall into a relationship.

The man in question tilted his head and considered her. "Since we're veering into the personal; what about you? Anything long term? I assume you're single since we're doing this fake thing."

"Like you, I've been too busy for anything longer than a couple of weeks here and there." She shrugged off his curiosity and she had no doubt he was curious. A woman her age, alone for years, was an anomaly. It wasn't that she'd lost a great love, she'd just lost a lot of small ones over time. She'd never had a deep heartbreak, but tiny cracks over years added up. She'd become cautious and wary. Still hopeful, but less enthusiastic.

"Busy with what?" Suddenly he seemed interested again, as if the mystery of a single woman in her thirties was something that needed solving. Right. Now.

"I don't know," she muttered. "Stuff. Life." She didn't want to get into all this.

"You've never moved away. Obviously, you're ambitious." He indicated her tablet. "Yet you never harbored aspirations to go to a big city to make your mark?"

His gaze sharpened on hers and she couldn't look away. He pulled at her, drew her in and she found herself leaning toward him again, caught in his need to know. She opened her lips to speak, but what was there to say? She couldn't be bothered? She'd become weary and leery of dating? Looking for a serious relationship had become a chore. Putting herself out there had become too much work. Especially since turning thirty.

But lately, she'd been aware of wasting those same years. Those early thirties.

She shook off the desire to explain her decision to set aside that part of herself. Instead, she focused on the other half of his version of her. The scared-to-try small town girl version.

"You think I'm scared to try my hand elsewhere? Is that it?" Frowning, she went on before he could respond. "Maybe I don't want to set the world on fire, just my little corner of it. And, yes, I know it's a *little* corner."

So much for small talk. Somehow, they'd moved from minutiae to deeper things. She shifted to shrug off his stabbing questions.

He leaned back but kept his hand on the bottom edge of his glass. His fingers were long and blunt, with square tips. Great hands.

"I'm sorry, I seem to have hit a nerve," he said unrepentantly. "I have a habit of doing that without realizing it until it's too late. Veronica used to hook her baby finger with mine when I got too intense at parties or events where I needed to be on my best behavior."

And he'd lost Veronica. Her support. That love. He'd lost his one true love and Farren was giving him a hard time over some silly questions.

"Excuse me," she said and rose to go to the ladies' room. She had to get a grip. Reminding him of his dead fiancée was a horrible thing to do. Even if she hadn't meant to do it, the hurt was real.

HE'D HATED THAT VERONICA had tried to rein him in, hoping to change him or make him more civilized. There had been times at social gatherings when he'd been deliberately testing someone or looking for a weakness in a plan. She'd hook her finger to his and *tsk*. Then she'd change the subject, making him lose his advantage. Asking pointed questions was often the best way to get to the meat of a problem. Countless times, she'd interrupted his train of thought, and the moment had been lost.

At first, he'd appreciated that she was looking out for him during those times when he got too deeply involved in conversations. Social situations had always been minefields. Until Veronica, he'd avoided them. She'd convinced him that making an appearance and chatting inanely would help O'Hara grow.

He was sorry he'd made Farren feel awkward here in the sunshine and the cool ocean breeze. She should never feel awkward. She had ambition and drive, but it was small-time and small town. He'd never be happy being a big fish in a little pond. Frankly, he didn't see how Singles Fest could stay small and survive. She needed to take it to a global market.

He sipped at his beer and ruminated.

A few minutes went by where he closed his eyes and raised his face to the sun, thinking.

A chair grated and Farren settled back into her seat with a brief smile that lifted her mouth, but not her face. Not her usual smile at all.

"Farren," he said gently, "you're far from scared. You're smart and ambitious and thorough. I'm curious why a woman with your attributes would choose to remain in such a sleepy town. From what I see, nothing's changed for the locals. Still no schools, nothing but tourist shops. They may change hands, but they don't grow."

She stared at him, waiting for the punchline, he guessed.

"Last Chance Beach is not a place to build a business." Some of the storefronts had had facelifts. But the place was far from bustling. "People retire here and buy a small business to have something to do. No one's making bank that way."

She drew in a deep breath. "Maybe it's not a place to build a brick-and-mortar business, but that's not what I'm doing. I'm building a business that will have international appeal. Did you know there's a festival in Ireland that's gone on for hundreds of years? It's dedicated to singles looking for marriage. That's the sole reason for its existence." She straightened and gave him a 'take that' look.

"And now we come to the reason I pressed you," he said, happy to hear she'd been thinking globally. "I was sure you must have a deeper understanding of what you want to achieve. Lots of people have trouble expressing their innermost thoughts. I put you on the spot at my place last night. I made you fumble and then I proposed this ridiculous fake dating thing. That must've thrown you right off your game."

She shifted her shoulders. "Sort of. I guess." She looked past his shoulder. "The food's on the way."

He had a special request of the server.

"Vinegar?" Farren asked as the server moved off to fulfill his request.

"For fish and chips, yes."

For a few minutes, they fell to silence as another couple settled their bill at the next table. When the vinegar had been delivered, they added their condiments, vinegar included. She watched him sprinkle it on his fish and chips and rolled her eyes. She dabbed a fry into her ketchup blob.

"I picked up the habit in England. Try a fry." He held out a perfectly deep-fried sample and waited while she considered whether to eat from his hand or not. She leaned in, opened her mouth and he placed the vinegar-dipped fry between her beautifully lush lips.

She chewed, swallowed, and smiled. "That's good. Huh. Who'd have thought?"

"The Brits. Now, put some on your fish, too."

"Okay, I'm in," she said and gave him the real smile he'd been waiting for.

They finished their meal and as she wiped her lips with her napkin, her eyes went serious. "I'm sorry I made you think of Veronica. You said she was off limits and I'm afraid I led you to talking about a painful memory."

"You have nothing to apologize for," he said and made a mental note to check out the Irish Festival she'd mentioned. He didn't want to press her for anything now. He'd have plenty of time later. Suddenly, hanging out with Farren and watching Singles Fest come to fruition felt as if it could be...fun.

It had been years since having fun had been a priority. He'd spent his life seeing the world as a serious place. Fun, in and of itself, had never been a goal. He looked into Farren's wide purply-blue eyes and saw weeks full of laughter waiting in their depths. Maybe this was what he needed to get himself back on track.

And a kiss or two might help.

Chapter Eight

THE NEXT AFTERNOON, at the Landseer, Farren looked out toward the beach and saw a head bob up and down. A broad pair of shoulders soon appeared as well. Grady. Was he? Yes, he was. She smiled and headed for the walkway to talk to her handyman who looked busy being handy.

As she stepped off the lawn and onto the wooden boards, she caught her breath at the sight of Grady, on his hands and knees with a hammer in his hand and two nails between his lips. *Oh, my.*

His shirt was open, his face glistened and as she watched, he swiped his forearm across his brow. She had to gather herself before speaking. She'd seen newspaper photos of him in a tuxedo, so she knew he killed the sophisticated look, but this was completely different.

Farren blinked slowly three times and still the image of that forearm lingered. She swallowed and opened her mouth.

"Hello! Do you need a cold drink? It's hot out here."

Grady raised his head to look at her, his eyes trailing from the top of her head to her bare toes. "It's hot, all right, but I came prepared." He pointed to an insulated aluminum bottle.

"Oh, good." She stepped closer, admiring the work he'd done so far. "This will be finished in no time." New, freshly sawn wooden planks interspersed with older ones and the job looked about half done and it was only eleven a.m. "When did you get out here?"

"I wanted to start before the heat of the day, so six-thirty. I'll be quitting soon. The sun's too strong, even with sunscreen." He leaned back on his heels and looked up at her. "I'll be going for a swim soon. Care to join me?"

She thought of running home to grab her suit and towel. Thought of bobbing in the waves with Grady only feet away and next to naked. Her nipples firmed, but it was the thought of the cold water that gave her the reaction. *Sure, it was.*

"I shouldn't," she demurred. "I have so much to do, and a swim would mean showering again and drying my hair for my meeting this afternoon."

"Don't say I didn't invite you."

"I really wish I could. How about later?"

"No can do. I'll be online with Tokyo." He made a face. "Another time. Maybe when Delphine's on the way over. We can put on a show for her."

"Share a kiss in the water?" she blurted and stepped back. She shouldn't have let her fantasy show up in this conversation. *Step away from the man in the toolbelt.* Her belly fluttered and a thrill shot through her.

"Something like that." He flashed her a grin that promised a world full of thrills. And probably hurt when he went back to New York.

"Well, I came out here to say that the bath refitting company says they can get the three units finished this week."

"Let's hope they keep to the schedule and stay on budget." And there he was, the grouch. Growly and demanding when there was no need to be. She'd just told him the company was on target and on schedule. Their prices were fair, and she'd been given a discount because once they were on site, there was no travel time from one unit to the next.

She spun on her heel and tramped back to the motel. Next up on her list was a quick lunch in her car and then a run out to Barnacle Bill's. She could have asked Grady to join her, but that would mean waiting for him to finish and clean up. She couldn't miss her appointment with Tom Fester and since Grady was feeling growly, she might do better with Tom on her own. She'd flash her eyes and give him her best smile. Couldn't hurt.

TWO DAYS LATER, FARREN was having drinks at The Sandbar Bar and Grill in the Sands with Eva. It was a typical hotel bar except that the whole wall that faced the beach was glass. Today, the sliders were wide open to catch the breeze and salt air. Beautiful, the view never failed to make her smile. She loved living in a place where she could have days like this.

In the evenings, small groups took tables inside and out on the patio.

They'd taken a table in the back so they could talk privately. So far, all she'd done was answer questions about Grady. Endless questions, it seemed. She'd invited Eva so she could give her an update on Singles Fest, but her friend wanted to talk about Grady. Farren had just explained how she'd bullied her way into his place the night they'd met.

"And how did you end up on a lunch date?"

"Despite looking like a shaggy mess, Grady was funny and charming, but I had to convince him that I was onto something with Singles Fest." All of which was true except for the funny and charming part. "I waited for him the next morning so we could go through the units together and when he arrived home from his errands, he'd cleaned up so well I thought he must be someone else."

"You didn't recognize him? Wow, he must've been a hairy beast."

"With holes in his socks," she added for good measure. "But the man who showed up the next morning looked crisp and fresh and...." No, she couldn't go there.

"Handsome? Because he looked great when I saw you with him at lunch." Eva waggled her eyebrows like a lech. "Hubba hubba."

Farren laughed. "Nobody says that anymore. And men shouldn't be objectified any more than women."

The eyebrow waggling continued. "Don't distract me. The man's gorgeous. And not just physically. He seems smart and kind. And interested in you. Also, he's dated models and actresses in New York and LA. Everyone's seen his photos." She grinned and sipped her wine. "And you know exactly what hubba hubba means. We both had grandmothers, right?"

Eva's amusement was contagious. "Mm, yes. I do know what hubba hubba means. Grady cleaned up is not what I expected." She grinned. "To be honest I didn't expect him to clean up at all. So when he suggested a stroll on the beach to get lunch, I agreed." Simple lies were best. "Delphine hasn't seen him in months, and I doubt she knows how badly he'd let himself go." She assumed he'd cleaned up because they'd be seen in public. His sudden interest in grooming had nothing to do with impressing her and everything to do with his public image.

"How bad was he? Lone bomber scary or just run-of-the-mill grieving man shaggy?"

"Never mind about that," Farren said with some force, sorry she'd mentioned anything about his bear-in-the-woods look. "I was hoping if Grady helped with Singles Fest, then his sister would, too." Another lie. *Sheesh.*

"I decided to sit up on The Rock to eat my fish and chips," Eva announced smugly. "You two looked like quite the happy couple from there. You clasped hands across the table and then shared your fries. I saw him feed you one."

"You spied on us?"

"Everyone sits on The Rock to eat their take-out."

She hadn't looked around much that day. She'd been focused on Grady. "He wanted me to taste the vinegar he puts on his fish and chips." Sitting on The Rock meant perching on the side of a boulder the height of a bungalow. No one could remember The Rock's real color because for decades it had been the place to announce undying love and affection. Periodically the town painted over the names, dates, and love interests and provided a fresh canvas. And every time, a parade of older citizens scampered over the granite to replace what was lost. Now, there was talk of sandblasting all the layers of paint off to return the rock to pristine.

Newcomers. They wanted to change things. The Rock was perfect as it was. A landmark. She saw no reason to change it just because new people wanted to make their mark on the town.

Farren believed, like most of the longtime residents, that giving lovestruck people a place to tell the world about their love was romantic. And it saved other landmarks from being tagged.

"Okaaayyy. It looked lovey-dovey from where I sat."

She'd be sure to tell Grady they'd put on a good show next time she saw him. Whenever that would be. They hadn't made plans after that lunch. She'd only seen him working on the walkway. And she hadn't been to the motel since she'd shown the bathtub refitting company the units they needed updated. So much for faking a relationship.

She gave a mental shrug, to dislodge the memory of Grady in a toolbelt with his shirt open and his forearms looking so strong. She'd see him again at some point.

"I invited you here to talk about the list of outings I have in mind for Singles Fest, not gossip about Grady." Even if he was a grump of the highest order, he didn't deserve to be fodder for derisive comments. Or giggles. Or feminine speculation.

But Eva looked ready to press her for more information when a deep male voice interrupted them.

"Hey there," a man said from over Eva's shoulder. Eva turned to face the man. "Would you mind if my friend and I join you?" he asked her with a smooth, engaging smile. Tall, dark-haired, and interested. A second man stood just behind the one who'd spoken.

"That depends," Farren replied before Eva could send them on their way. It would be a relief to change the topic from Grady. "What is your purpose in joining us?"

Eva turned back to face her with a frown.

The men flanking Eva smiled widely. In fact, the man who'd spoken looked happy to answer Farren's pointed question.

"Our purpose. Hm...having a drink and some lively conversation with two lovely women?" he said it like he was guessing and hoping Farren and Eva wanted the same thing.

He wore boaters, white shorts, and looked great in a light blue cotton shirt. The other man was dressed similarly except his shirt was navy linen. They were around the same age. Mid-thirties if she had a bet riding on it.

"Let me guess," Farren said. "You're here for some beach time, golf, and whatever else you can find to do in sleepy little Last Chance Beach." Farren smiled gently because tourists wanted to feel welcome and indulged. "Fair enough." She gave Eva a look of approval.

Eva indicated a couple of chairs at another table. "Pull those over and we'll include you in our lively conversation," she said with a look for Farren that promised retribution.

"Archie Jones," the first man said as he took a chair and set it beside Farren. His friend landed in the chair next to Eva with a sigh.

"I'm Jesse Carmichael," the friend said. "Are we interrupting?" He waved at the women's tablets. "This looks like a business meeting."

"You're not interrupting at all. In fact, I'd like to pick your brains, if you don't mind." Farren pulled her tablet toward her to give them more room on the table for drinks. Archie smiled his thanks and waved for the server. This was perfect. Not only could she discuss her plans with Eva, but she could get a male perspective at the same time.

She'd planned on talking this out with Grady, but so much for being seen in public together. One lunch and done.

Eva watched the men with amusement. But Farren noticed her friend's eye caught on Jesse's more than once. That meant Farren should focus on Archie.

"You want to pick our brains?" Jesse asked Eva. Her gaze snagged on his and pink rose in her cheeks.

Taking note of the obvious attraction, Farren opened her tablet to her profile questionnaire. "Yes, a few questions," she said. "Nothing serious or onerous. You're both single?"

They nodded and smiled.

She opened two files, one for each man. "Have you been married or in a long-term relationship before? Something serious?"

At the question, Archie looked at Jesse. "Not me, yet."

Jesse nodded. "Yes, I was married, but I'm a widower. Two years ago." He blew out a long breath as if he'd carried the burden as far as he wanted to.

The women offered their condolences, but they were cut short by the arrival of the men's drinks.

Eva watched Jesse with deep sympathy in her gaze. After the server retreated, she said, "That must be terrible."

"It's my kids I worry about."

Farren tossed Eva a look that screamed between them. A widower with kids counted as a single dad. She cleared her throat. "How many children?" she asked.

"Three," he responded. "Two girls and a boy."

"If you don't mind me asking, where are they while you're here?" Farren typed quickly.

"I was lucky because my in-laws agreed to take them. They're busy people so this weekend away is a real break." Jesse's face grew curious. "Why?"

"You walked over here to join two women for drinks. Are you looking for a relationship? Or just a good time?" She leaned in and then back when she realized she must look like a hungry baby bird begging for scraps.

He flashed her a strong smile that showed he was down for sharing. "First, it was Archie who led the charge. Second, did you miss the part where I said I have three kids?" He chuckled. "There's no way for me to find a relationship if I wanted to. Who's going to take on another woman's children? One, maybe, but three? They're young and need a lot of time and attention. So, looking for a relationship is not on my agenda."

Jesse flashed Eva a look, but she was gazing at the tabletop and missed it. In fact, Eva seemed to have shriveled into her seat. Her face had gone stony, and Jesse looked accepting when he read her expression.

Whatever spark of interest had been there for Eva had been snuffed out. It was obvious that his having children had made her withdraw. He was likely right. Finding a new relationship would be incredibly difficult for a man like Jesse.

Confused by her friend's reaction, Farren knew she'd have to work fast to get through her questions. She cleared her throat.

"Would a woman having children put either of you off dating her?"

Archie shrugged and looked unconcerned. "Not necessarily. Especially if they were old enough to do stuff with, like going to games or bowling or other fun things."

"Have you dated a woman with children?"

Archie flushed. "Yes, but not for long. The kids were too young. Diapers and car seats are not my thing."

Jesse gave his buddy a disapproving look. "Archie here is all about the good time."

Archie sipped his beer and shrugged. "I might hang out with a kid who was old enough to have fun with. Do things with. Just because I haven't doesn't mean it's completely off the table."

Eva spoke up. "Things like minigolf?" She nodded at Farren, who still hadn't convinced Barnacle Bill's to offer her groups a discount.

Jesse looked aggrieved by his friend's comments. "Kids aren't all fun and games," he grumbled. "Kids need people they can depend on."

"And you, Jesse?" Farren asked. "Would you have room for a woman's children?"

"I guess. But they'd have to like my kids." He sipped his beer and frowned. "That's a whole other layer of like, you know?"

Farren agreed.

"These are some strange questions," Jesse said.

Farren smiled to reassure the men. "You've both been very forthcoming and kind, so I'll let you in on what's happening."

Archie shared a look with Jesse. "We're all ears."

"I'm starting a dating site with a series of get-togethers and long weekends planned for single parents, so I want to include children's activities where the parents can meet and mingle."

"And the kids can, too?" Jesse finished for her, his eyes lighting.

"Exactly."

"I operate a daycare," Eva explained. "There would be options if parents wanted time off to be with another adult."

"Dates, you mean?" Archie, this time.

Eva nodded, but Farren spoke. "I'm planning things like dinners for the parents where they'd change tables through the meal. Typical evening singles events, but with the addition of family activities during the day."

Jesse considered the information then perked up. "I could bring the kids and have fun with them, but time for myself, too?" His gaze swung once more to Eva who gave him a brusque nod.

Farren spoke, since it was plain that her friend had lost the power of speech. "You've got it. Think something like this would interest you?"

"Sign me up," Jesse said with a wide grin. "Even if I didn't meet a woman for me, it sounds like a great way to spend a weekend. Would it be here?"

"Yes, for now."

"And Eva would handle daycare and the kids' activities when I'd be out with the other parents?"

Eva nodded. "I'll have babysitters lined up."

Both men nodded but Archie looked bored.

"If things go as well as I hope, I'll expand to each coast and up north on the Great Lakes. I think beach towns are perfect for this idea."

"Here's to success!" Jesse toasted and held up his glass. They all cheered until a dark shadow loomed over the table from directly behind her.

Farren looked up into the disgruntled blue eyes of her fake boyfriend.

GRADY TRIED TO KEEP it light and smile engagingly, but he was pretty sure he missed the mark when Farren paled. "Farren, I didn't expect to see you here," he said with a nod for Eva. "Nice to see you again, Eva."

He'd walked into the bar looking for a quick lunch and a cold beer. From the back tables he'd heard animated conversation that drew his attention. Surprised by the source, he watched for a couple of minutes. When Farren started waving her hands and smiling, he'd edged closer. Those smiles she was tossing around were her real ones. His favorite.

Now, he was making himself a fool by glaring at her. Her smile drifted away, and her hands settled on the table. "Grady."

No inflection good or bad. No sign of welcome.

He blinked and tried for a more friendly demeanor. "And you are?" he directed the question to the men who had *tourist* written across their foreheads. The boaters were a dead giveaway.

"I'm Archie and this is Jesse," said the one next to Farren. "We just sat down." His tone asked, 'you got a problem?' Now, that was some good inflection.

"Care to join us? We're discussing Singles Fest," Farren said. "Jesse is a single dad and Archie is not."

"So, this is a focus group?" Sounded fishy to him, but whatever. He grabbed a chair from another table and squeezed into the space between Farren and Archie. "If you want input from a focus group, don't you need some single moms, too?"

"This was impromptu," Farren replied, while Eva looked ready to burst into laughter. "Archie and Jesse happened by and—."

"Oh, I get it," Grady interjected. He waved at the server for a beer. "Two beautiful women in a bar, two guys here for a weekend of beach and golf. Magnets." He shrugged and slipped his palm up to cup Farren's shoulder.

He probably should have walked out when he realized it was Farren cozied up in the back of the bar with these guys. But that might hurt their plan to convince Delphine they were dating. Satisfaction settled his mind. He was here now and here he'd stay.

He leaned in and kissed her cheek, startling her. He drew in her scent and sighed inside. He'd missed this. Looks like he didn't need to get Delphine to hang around after all. He could fake kiss Farren in front of anyone.

"Uh, right." She patted his hand where it sat on her shoulder and smiled up at him as if she meant it. The smile punched him in the gut.

"The bathrooms are being done today. They look good," he said into Farren's ear. She nodded.

"Great," she said. "Grady owns the Landseer Motel and I'll be offering special rates to families who attend our weekends. He has the biggest pool and best playground in Last Chance Beach."

Jesse nodded. "My kids will love that. My boy's learning to swim but the girls are like fish."

Eva shifted uncomfortably. "I'm a certified lifeguard so I'll be there with the children if the parents go off for adult events."

"That's a shame you don't get to have any fun," Jesse said with a warm smile for Eva. Eva looked blindly at the tabletop.

"Eva loves children," Farren said.

"How do you feel about kids?" Grady asked her. Personally, he wanted a couple, but until now, he hadn't seen himself with any. Maybe he'd been expecting Veronica to decide. He frowned, unsure what her position on children had been. They'd never discussed having a family and as of six weeks ago, he knew why.

Funny, the rage he'd lived with for these weeks had faded to a dull acceptance. Things would never have been right with Veronica. She'd never given them a chance.

Chapter Nine

FARREN TURNED HER HEAD toward Grady. Since he'd bussed her cheek, his face was still kissing close. He'd asked her feelings about having children. She stared into his blue, blue eyes and the rest of the group fell away.

"You're asking me that now? Seems a little soon, don't you think?" Grady's eyes, so close, his clean-shaven chin firm and with his perfect cheekbones, previously hidden behind a scruff of facial hair. The man was devastating. At least, to her.

"Time's ticking for me," Grady said softly. "I don't want to be too old to toss a football around when my kids are teens. I'd also like to win at hoops once in a while."

He was fishing and bluffing and pushing this fake thing to the wall. She wasn't sure why since his sister wasn't here, but she could play along. Maybe this was all for Eva's sake.

"Yes, I feel the same way. Time's drifting by for me, too. But first, I need to get this baby up and running. By baby I mean Singles Fest."

"I know what you meant." Seemingly satisfied, Grady pulled back and settled into his seat.

Farren blinked and the others at the table came into focus. Archie and Jesse were sipping their beer and looking toward the front of the bar, while Eva was holding in a chuckle. She shook her head with mirth.

"Where were we?" Farren asked.

"We were discussing the children's activities," Jesse provided. "I'm ready to sign up now."

"Really? That's wonderful. I'm taking email addresses for a waiting list. You'll be hearing back as soon as we launch. For now, I'm trying to create buzz online."

"My brother's wife is an influencer with a decent following of moms. She focuses on self-care for busy mothers. I could mention it to her." This, from Archie who snagged Farren's and Eva's attention with his comment.

"She'd have single moms following her," Farren realized aloud. She smiled right into Archie's eyes. "You'd be my new best friend if you could help me out."

Her smile stretched wide, and excitement wrapped its arms around her. Or was that Grady sharing her joy by draping a possessive arm over her? From the accepting look on Archie's face, it was Grady, laying claim again.

And she was oddly okay with that. She leaned into the former grizzly next to her and he squeezed her affectionately.

Eva clapped with excitement. She and Jesse shared a look. "You wanted lively conversation and look what's happened."

"DO YOU HAVE BARNACLE Bill's onboard yet?" Grady asked Farren.

She shook her head. "I keep meaning to go to see Tom Fester again, but last time he made it clear he doesn't want to give up any profit. I understand. Maybe he'll offer a deal another time. Maybe during the shoulder season." People who weren't tied to the school year for their vacations provided shoulder seasons. They visited Last Chance Beach in the spring and early autumn to avoid the summer rush.

"Have you tried talking to his grandfather?"

"No, Bill Fester retired a few years ago."

"But he still owns the park. And Bill was a particular friend of Aunt Ellen's." He wagged his eyebrows at her.

"Oh?" Her eyes widened. "Oh! I didn't know that."

He pulled out his phone and called. "Bill? This is Grady O'Hara."

LATER, AT HIS PLACE, Grady enjoyed the sight of Farren standing by the kitchen window, the pink light of sunset giving her a glow. His phone interrupted the small talk they'd been engaged in since walking back from The Sandbar. "It's Delphine."

"Take the call, Grady. She misses you."

"Okay. I'll take it for you," he said and was glad he did because a wide smile broke out on her pretty face.

"What's happened, Grady?" Delphine demanded on the phone. "You answered my call. What's wrong?" Concern leaked from his sister's voice into his ear. He shifted, stifling the effect her worry had on him. Maybe he'd been too harsh in ghosting her. Ignoring her calls had been churlish. And now she was worried.

But he still didn't want to tell her everything. Not yet. Maybe never.

"Nothing's wrong," he replied. "You called and I answered. I know it's been a while, but I had some stuff to sort out. On my own. Not everything is up for discussion or dissection." Especially not with a sister who wanted to run his life.

She sniffed. "You haven't taken a call from me in weeks."

Six weeks, he thought, but didn't say. Delphine would be devastated if she knew what he'd learned. His sister could be a royal pain, but she didn't deserve to be punished for wanting to see him married and settled. And clearly, Veronica had faked her out, too. Best to let the sad revelations end right here.

He glanced at Farren who was studiously pretending not to eavesdrop.

He should take pity on his worrywart sister. Not long ago, he'd have turned the screws out of pique. She had a lot to answer for, but he didn't see a time when he'd ever tell her the truth about Veronica.

"Farren's here," he said to answer her "what happened" question. "We were having drinks at the Sandbar, then we walked home. I'm about to grill some burgers. Was there something you needed to tell me?"

"Farren's with you? Great. Why didn't you say so?"

"I just did."

"Well, then, there's nothing I need to say. Have a nice evening." She hung up.

"That was quick." Farren quipped.

"Yes. She apparently called for no reason. Which never happens. There's a reason for everything Delphine does."

"You make her sound like a schemer."

"Let's just say being her brother gives me a clearer perspective." He ran his hand over his hair.

"Huh," she said softly and turned to face him. "Are you really grilling me a burger or was that a ruse to get Delphine off the phone?"

"I thought we'd check out the job done on the bathrooms and then eat. I'll drive you home later unless you'd prefer me to walk you home."

"I can walk on my own."

"And what would Delphine say about me letting my date walk home alone?" He grinned and held the door open for her.

"This wasn't a date. Remember? You walked into the bar and found me there. A coincidence." She passed through the door, brushing by him as she moved.

"A happy coincidence," he pointed out. Especially since he was able to give that Archie the signal to look elsewhere. Also, he'd been wondering where she'd been the last couple of days. Not that he'd been scouting around for her. No. He hadn't done that. She'd been busy with all the social media she'd been developing. Not his area of expertise, so he'd left her to it. "We haven't seen each other much."

"True, but we're both busy," she said with a breeze in her voice. "It was useful to talk to Archie and Jesse. I got great feedback and Archie's sister-in-law will be a real boost. She's on several platforms and will be an asset. Too bad she's happily married and won't need my services, or I would offer her a freebie."

"I'll give her a weekend at the motel if she wants. If she's got kids, I'm sure the family will have a good time."

She turned to face him; her face pleased and happy with him. If this whole thing was real, he'd open his arms and she might walk into them for a thank you hug. "Would you really give them a free room?"

But it wasn't real, so he kept his arms at his sides. "Of course. If she has the Singles Fest experience with her family, she'll have firsthand knowledge and use it for good. Apparently, some influencers have superpowers."

He could get his marketing people onboard with a few well-placed posts and online ads. Couldn't hurt. "We have a new intern, I'll set him to work."

He opened the door to the first unit. As before, the beds were bare, but the mattresses looked clean and fresh. "The air's fresher. Nice job," he said and headed to check on the bathroom. "Happy?" he asked as he indicated she should look for herself.

She leaned into the doorway to see. Again, she was close, and he was tempted to touch, but kept his hands to himself. "Yes, it looks great. Exactly what we're after," she said.

On the way to the other units, they strolled beside the pool. The gentle lap of the water soothed as the breeze kicked up. "After we eat, we could have a swim." He repeated his request from the other day.

"No suit," she replied blithely. Her arched brow said skinny dipping was out of the question.

"This could be our last chance to have the pool to ourselves."

"I'll bring a suit over tomorrow."

"Do that." But he doubted she would. Maybe she was shy about showing herself. But she was born and raised here. The beach and swimming were second nature.

"O'Hara Enterprises' new intern is all over the internet. Nice kid and seems to know his stuff." Grady wasn't up on the newest platforms. Having gone to ground for six months meant he was behind and that was fine with him. His time here had convinced him he'd been too splintered to be effective before. Even with an assistant as effective as Veronica. He'd reassessed everything since her death, and more in recent weeks.

"An intern has time to help me? You're sure?"

"Probably. I'll check. If not, I'll have HR find you one. I'm sure there's an eager beaver looking for a placement with a start-up online dating service."

"You think?"

"Especially if you offer a ground floor opportunity. A stake in the company."

She frowned. "I don't know. I'd have to think hard about that."

"Suit yourself. At this point, it wouldn't cost you anything and later, when the business grows, you'll have built-in loyalty and that counts for a lot."

"What happened to the man who didn't want to let me into his house or listen to what I had to say?" She crossed her arms and tilted her head as if discovering a new species of insect. The teasing light in her eyes warmed him.

He laughed out loud. "That guy? Woke up." He patted his chest. "I swear I've changed."

"How? What changes have occurred since holing up at the Landseer?"

"I learned to delegate. And the world didn't collapse." It was true. He had good people working for him and for the good of O'Hara.

"Amazing."

"I think so." He wanted to laugh at the lightening of his soul, and he had Farren to thank. "Let me grill you the best burger you've ever eaten."

"I'll be the judge of that."

"You're a cheeky thing, but you're right. You will judge my burgers by all that have come before." He chuckled and held out his hand. She took it and let him tug her into a walk. Her hand felt warm and soft in his. So simple. Handholding. He absorbed the simplicity of the connection. "Before I fire up the grill, I want to show you what I've been up to for the past couple of days." He took her toward the freshly painted play equipment. When he twined his fingers with hers, she allowed it. And they didn't even have an audience. Warmth stole through his chest. "I painted here. The equipment looked sun bleached."

The playground looked bright and fun with primary colors glistening in the pearly light of dusk.

"Thanks for doing that. I could have helped. I've painted before," she said, looking delighted.

"Wait 'til you see the walkway." He kept her moving toward the beach.

"You've finished already?"

"I extended it and added a platform on one side for people who have difficulty navigating on the sand. Seniors or people pushing strollers, or the disabled can sit there and enjoy the sights and sounds of people on the beach."

"Oh, Grady, that's so thoughtful." She flushed the most beautiful pink. It rose from her chest and up her neck. He waited for a kiss to thank him, but it didn't come.

Chapter Ten

"THIS IS THE BEST BURGER I've ever eaten," Farren admitted an hour after Grady had shown her the rebuilt walkway with the viewing deck. He was considerate of the needs of less-mobile people and that had surprised her. Beaches were great but only if walking was easy for the people on them. His humble kindness had touched her.

But his humility had not extended to his culinary skills. He'd bragged unashamedly about his burgers. She chewed and swallowed another delicious bite.

They sat on the balcony over the veranda. He had a wrought iron café set here. A small, intricately designed table and two heavy straight-back chairs that didn't encourage lounging. But the view was spectacular from the second floor. And then it clicked. This fancy little table set was a leftover from his aunt. He'd brought Farren up here to enjoy the relaxing view.

She preferred not to think about how they'd walked through his bedroom to get here. "This is a lovely spot for morning coffee."

"I forget it's here half the time. Mostly, I swig coffee at the dining room table in front of my laptop."

"I'm glad you thought of coming up here, then." The breeze caught wisps of her hair and she tucked them behind her ears. She'd thrown together a Caesar salad and watched as he'd mixed a combination of beef and pork to make the burgers. He'd added a spice concoction of his own making.

"Are you sure you're not a chef? Or maybe a short order cook?" He could've put himself through college by grilling burgers. A painter, carpenter and cook, Grady O'Hara was a man of many talents.

The buns were fresh from the bakery, and he'd clearly hit the farmer's market in Summerville for the crisp romaine lettuce. Looking at his eager expression as he watched her reaction to his food, you'd never believe he was the same man she'd met a few days ago. Whatever had changed for Grady, she approved. He'd become friendly, open, and helpful and not at all like the grumpy bear he'd been.

"Not a chef, but my mom was a good cook and she liked to teach me because she said I was a good listener. Delphine, not so much." He shook his head.

She chuckled. "I wonder if my brothers are as opinionated about me."

"Do you interfere in their lives? Try to set them up with women you don't want?"

Unwanted women like her. She shook her head. "I never set them up. They're older. But I do have one who's going through a divorce." Ben had married too young, too wildly and he and his wife had been apart for more than a year. "Maybe I could find someone for him?"

"Don't. It won't end well."

She frowned. They were treading dangerous waters. He'd lost the love of his life and Delphine had been the one to set them up. But Veronica drowning on a dark lake could hardly be laid at his sister's feet. Farren decided to keep the conversation away from his past and on her future. Anything to ease his burden of grief.

"But isn't that what I'm proposing with Singles Fest? That I play matchmaker to the most vulnerable group of singles?"

"Vulnerable?" He spoke after a good chew and held his burger in both hands.

"Sure." She wiped her chin because she was sure she had mustard on it. Or pickle juice. "For instance, Jesse's concern was for his children first. A person he dates must like his children and their children *have to* like his. There's way more at stake for a parent. When the stakes are that high it equals vulnerability."

"There's a lot to lose when kids are involved." Grady nodded, getting it. "Especially for a guy like Jesse whose wife has died. His kids have already dealt with the worst kind of loss. So, him finding a partner is delicate." He turned thoughtful.

"Jesse's children are still dealing with losing their mom and will have that loss for the rest of their lives."

He cocked his head, and she realized that Grady's mom had been right. He listened well. "Sounds like experience talking."

She sighed. "No, but a friend lost her dad young and it's still a problem today."

"Tell me about what else you've been up to since we last saw each other."

"I'm checking so much off my to-do list I can't believe it. My website's finished, my newsletter has been designed, my social media campaign is ready to launch." She tapped three fingertips. "With your intern to help, I'm ready to roll out."

"I'll get Delphine on it too."

"She's already offered. And so have all my friends and family. I'll send them posts and tweets and pictures in the morning."

"I had no idea you were so close to launching."

"Once I knew I had you onboard, it all became easier. I kept working, of course, but when the Landseer came into play, the last major obstacle disappeared."

He laughed at being described as an obstacle. "Would you have come to see me without Delphine's urging?"

"Eventually, I guess. But I hadn't considered the motel because of your aunt's passing and your—um, how to put this—."

"My grief?" He finished her awkward sentence in a kind tone.

She shifted in embarrassed discomfort. She'd brought them right back to his biggest sorrow. "I'm sorry. I shouldn't have mentioned anything."

"It's okay," he said. "The worst is over. To be honest, your arrival came at a good time. Wallowing is not a good look on anyone. It tends to turn men into grizzled old guys before their time."

She smiled at that, her embarrassment easing. He was being understanding and sweet.

"The truth is," he continued, "I don't know what I was grieving most. My soon-to-be-wife or the family we'd have made? Or the business future I'd mapped out with Veronica at my side? What we had was half business, half personal." He blew out a strong breath at the end.

Farren had no response. There was nothing to say to such an odd confession.

Grady wiped his face and hands with a napkin. Then he took a sip of his beer. "I think my grief was mixed up with anger. She shouldn't have gone out alone in a canoe in the dark. She should have worn a life jacket. Once I got over the shock, I got angry, and it made me feel *something* while I shut down the rest of the grieving process. Since my mom, I haven't had a lot of losses on the personal side or the business side of my life. I didn't know how to handle it. At fourteen, I was numb for a long time. And this time, too. But I'm not numb anymore."

The look he gave her was intent and spoke of rivers of want. He missed Veronica. Heck, he still missed his mom. Her heart squeezed for him.

This had been the longest speech she'd heard from him. And he'd explained a lot of what she'd seen when she'd first met him. The grumpiness, the shaggy bear, the rusty voice.

"I see." She picked her next words carefully. "Anger is one of the stages of grief. I'm glad you've moved on." She hoped the next stage was acceptance, but she didn't want to get too personal.

"Me, too. Moving on is exactly what I want."

From there they focused on their meal for a time. To Farren the silence was companionable, comfortable. A seagull flew overhead and cocked his head at an angle for a better look at their table. "Don't look now but we're under surveillance."

He chuckled. "Good thing we're close to finished."

She blushed. "It was so good. I'm full."

The bird made one more pass then rose on an updraft and soared away toward the beach. "As much as they're pests for diners, they're impressive in flight," Grady mused aloud. "I also admire their scrappiness. They'll take on anything in the sky."

"I meant to say this earlier, but I got distracted by someone bragging on their grilling skills," she teased. "The playground looks so fresh. Thanks for the paintjob." She'd thought to clean them with a brush and bucket of water, but the new look was much more inviting.

"It didn't take long. And you're welcome."

"The wooden walkway and viewing deck are fabulous. That job must have taken a lot of time." She hadn't meant to have him do all this manual labor. "I'd budgeted for some of this, you know." Impossible not to flash on the way he'd looked sweaty and strong while swiping his forearm across his brow.

"My motel, remember? And the work did me good. I haven't worked with my hands in too long. Cleared my head. And the walkway took most of the last few days," he said. "I have the splinters to prove it." He held up his palms.

"Thank you. It means a lot that you'd suffer splinters for me." She took her last bite of hamburger.

"I should thank you for getting me out of my house. Next week, I'm heading to New York for a few of days, maybe a week, and I'm looking forward to going."

"Oh, that'll be good. What did you do while you were here? About work, I mean." Delphine had told her the company had run smoothly for all the time her brother had "checked out."

"Virtual meetings, email. I was surprised at how simple it was to work from home." He shrugged.

"Delphine is based in New York. Will you see her?"

"Unless she shows up here first. Which is more likely now that I answered her call." His dry tone made her smile.

"I'm glad you did. It would be hard for a sister to have a brother refusing to see her. I'd hate it."

He nodded. "You'd never do anything to make a brother want to distance himself."

"True, I'm not pushy with my family. Live and let live." Farren dished up the last of the Caesar salad for Grady. "Finish this and I'll take care of tidying up."

"Deal." He forked up some salad, and then held the fork away from his mouth so he could speak. "When I'm gone the motel will be empty. Do you want to move in then?" He filled his mouth while waiting for her to consider his request.

She warmed at his suggestion. "You mean here? In the house or motel?"

"The Landseer." He chewed and swallowed before continuing. "We talked about you living in the unit next door. I thought having someone here while I'm gone would be a good idea." He frowned. "Unless you've changed your mind."

"I can move my own furniture in?" She loved her new bed and didn't want to store it. "I can use the table and chairs that are in there and if the beds are removed, I'll bring my own sofa and my new bed."

Grady nodded. "Both beds out, but the table and chairs stay. You need room for your sofa. Check." He nodded. "I'll handle it. What about the television?"

"It's fine. I won't watch much. I binge a show here and there, but I can do that on my computer."

"I'll move in a new television for you. You'll have all the channels and services." He said it as if it was a fait accompli and she had no say.

She thought of the obscenely huge television on his living room wall. "Not too big, please. The room's too small for a massive screen."

"Okay. What will happen with your accommodation now? Will you move back in, or will you have to move elsewhere when we're through?"

Practical. Grady was practical and looked to the future. "My landlord will offer my place for short term rentals. He already has furniture for it. Since he's my brother, I'll be allowed to move back in whenever I want."

He looked relieved. "Great. I'll give you the password for my wi-fi until we get the motel's system up and running." He finished his last bite of salad and then picked up his dirty dishes.

"Perfect," she rose, her plate and the salad bowl in her hands. She followed him through his bedroom, keeping her gaze away from his personal spaces. Mostly because she already knew the room was tidy just like the rest of the house.

Back in the kitchen, Grady opened the dishwasher for her, and they both added their dishes.

When he closed the door, they were standing inches apart. "I'll tell my sister you've moved in with me."

"You'll *what*?"

TELLING DELPHINE THEY'D moved in together seemed drastic. "What will my brothers think?" Farren demanded. "My parents?"

"That you're a grown up and are in a serious relationship."

"No, no, no." She shook her head and held up her hands. This wasn't like a new television. He couldn't just tell everyone she'd moved in with him. "That's not what we agreed. This was supposed to be a fake, casual dating thing. Not serious. No hearts involved. The breakup is supposed to be easy, with no heartbreak."

She didn't want to have to pretend to be *getting over* Grady. When the time came, she wanted to skim over the details of the break with him. Make it seem a mutual parting of the ways with no one hurt because no promises were made. Her brothers and parents would believe that because that's how Farren lived. Easy come and easy go with men. "Most of the time, my family doesn't meet the man I'm seeing."

"So, you're *always* in casual situations?"

She walked to the futon and picked up her bag for her walk home. "Yes. I'm a serial casual dater if you need to label me." Living at Last Chance Beach the choice was that or be alone. She didn't mind being alone, but once upon a time, she'd had dreams of something more and now those dreams had returned. Turning thirty-four, quitting her job and starting her own business had shifted her life and her future. Her old dreams had revved to life.

"And the world thinks *I* cut myself off," Grady muttered. "Let's walk and we'll come up with a plan to suit us both."

Instead of strolling the beach, they took to the road, a winding narrow strip that had been paved a long time ago. No sidewalk and gravel shoulders. Most people who walked it stayed in the middle because the sides were broken and dangerous traps for turned ankles.

The streetlights were few and far between, adding to the mystery of what lay in the ditches on either side.

They walked a few hundred yards before she spoke. "It's not that I want to be casual," she explained. "But living here means available men, decent men, are only here for the short-term. Sometimes I meet someone, and they come back to see me again. But most often, their lives keep them away and I like to think I become a pleasant memory of their time here."

"I'm getting an odd picture." He frowned in the gloaming, darker than the gathering night.

"It's not often that I meet someone I want to spend time with. But, if I never take a chance with anyone, I'll never have a partner. So, I take my chances without getting my hopes up." She wasn't going to admit to her re-awakened dreams. He might take the wrong meaning and decide she was after something more from him than their arrangement called for.

He nodded. "I get it. I was so involved in my business I fell into a similar pattern. Until Veronica, that is."

"I'm glad you found her. If you've been in love once, I'm sure you'll find it again," she responded gently. "And now, here we are, a pair of casual daters thrust together for convenience."

"For what it's worth, I'm having a good time getting to know you." He flashed her a smile that lit his face.

She let her fingers find his as they walked down the road toward the brighter lights of Main Street.

"I'll tell my brothers I'm in the motel unit, not your house." She wouldn't budge on this. "I'll also tell them we're casual, so they won't wander over to the Landseer to get in your face."

He chuckled. "Fine. But as far as Delphine goes, you live with me, and the unit is available to all staff members like a break room."

"Deal." She'd have offered her private space to Eva anyway.

GRADY LET THE MATTRESS slide from his hands into place on the box spring. Farren set her side down gently, too.

"There," he said, "that's the last of the heavy things. If you're sure the television is where you want it, then I can leave you to it." The rental moving trailer has empty but for her clothes and other small things, like lamps and a chair she used when she worked. "I'll grab your office chair for you. Will the kitchen table be okay for your workspace?"

Her whole face lit up as she surveyed the unit. "That's what I've always done, so it's fine. I dream of having a real home office someday. With a proper desk and a printer stand. Maybe a filing cabinet." She pouted, a pursing of her soft lips. "I've wanted one of those for a long time. They look so official."

His groin tightened as he thought of giving her all she wanted, and maybe all he wanted, too. Stupid to be turned on by a pout. But then they *were* standing beside a bed. And he was a man who hadn't...

"There's a spare room upstairs at the house you could use as real office space," he offered. "When Singles Fest takes off, you may need more room." And she may want to keep her personal space, personal.

"You're really onboard. I appreciate the vote of confidence." Her purply-blue gaze punched him in the gut again. He bet she had no idea how much he liked looking into her eyes. The smile that played around the corners of her mouth made him wonder how she'd taste. So far, they'd only bussed each other on the cheek. And that wasn't nearly enough.

"One thing I've learned working from home is to keep personal and office space as separate as you can. It's hard to shut off your work if it's sitting in front of you."

"But you work on the dining room table."

"That's how I know it's hard to shut down. After dinner last night, I moved my laptop into the den. Now I can shut the door on it." Not that it mattered much. He was leaving in the morning.

She dug a set of white sheets out of a box and tossed them on the bed. A couple of pillows followed. "Down time is rare when I'm swamped by my to-do list."

She flapped out a bottom sheet and he automatically grabbed a corner to hook it under the mattress.

"Thanks," she said, "but you don't have to help me make the bed." Her cheeks had pinkened with the intimacy of the homey gesture.

He raised his hands in surrender. "Yeah, right," he murmured and hooked a thumb over his shoulder. "I'll get the chair for you and be on my way."

"Thank you for all your help. Eva's busy, or she'd have been here to help, and my brothers don't know I've moved yet."

"Not even your landlord brother?"

"No. I'll tell him later today. Thanks again. This will make my life easier. Being close to the first wave of guests will give me better insight into what they want, need, and might prefer for next time." She snapped the top sheet out wide and let it drift down to land on the bed. "Thanks for your help today."

"Half an hour. It was nothing." He tossed her the key to his place. "This is in case of emergency, but I doubt anything will go wrong. I've already killed all the plants, so they don't need watering."

"I'll add it to the rest of the motel keys I carry." She went to the counter where she'd left the full key ring. "I'll park my car in front of your door, so it looks like someone's home."

"In case the roving bands of thieves Last Chance Beach is known for take an interest?" he joked. They had a new police department and the town had gone quiet. The beach parties had toned down a bit and he supposed some of the older residents felt safer, but he hadn't seen the need. More services meant more taxes. The older residents would be the first ones to complain when taxes went up.

"Yep. In case." She tucked her fingertips into the pockets of her cut-offs and rocked back on her heels. "We've even got people now who lock their doors." She raised her eyebrows, feigning shock. "Imagine."

"I can't." He stood like a dope staring at her. Farren's pretty features glowed in fading light from the window as she looked back at him, the expanse of half-made bed between them. Her flowing pink top rose and fell with each breath, like silk. She'd tied her hair up in a loose knot that threatened to tumble to her shoulders. He loved the look. Simple and small town. And so sexy he could hardly breathe. "Maybe you don't have to tell your family. You were concerned what they'd think."

She pursed her lips. "My brother will tell for sure. He's a suck up when it comes to tattling, especially on me." She grimaced. "And this arrangement may not be for long. I could hate living here with the families. I'm used to quiet and live away from the beach. I'll stay for high season because I'll be needed, but I'm not sure I'll stay longer."

"Thanks for agreeing to stay here at all. I'd have to move out if guests started banging on my door whenever they had a problem." They'd been over all this, but he couldn't seem to make his feet move to leave her.

"You still have no idea how long you'll be away?"

"I'll know more when I get there." He'd planned for a few days, but he could get sucked back into the day-to-day. "I also need to hire a new assistant. Someone of my own choosing this time." Delphine had made some noises about finding him a replacement for Veronica, but he'd put her off. Too awkward.

He didn't want a replacement assistant *and* a replacement, *fake* girlfriend. Seeing a new woman in Veronica's role felt like too much. Next time, he'd aim for a male assistant just to make the transition easier.

Farren's gaze fell to the bed. "I should finish this. I still have a lot to do."

"Right. One chair coming up." He turned on his heel and made his last trip to the trailer and returned with the chair. He set it down, blew out a breath and said, "See you when I see you, then."

"See you," she said with a wan smile and a wave. The bed was ready, and she was busy unloading cans of food and boxes of cereal into the two kitchen cabinets. The mini fridge had been filled earlier.

He had a thought that he should reassure her that he'd come back, but what if he didn't? What if O'Hara Enterprises wrapped itself around him again?

Chapter Eleven

AT DAWN THE NEXT MORNING, Grady drove over the Last Chance Beach bridge to the mainland, satisfied with his decision to leave the motel in Farren's hands. She was capable and invested in taking care of the place. Almost like a partner. She'd accepted the help of the office intern with her social media marketing and her brand was shaping up nicely.

The more he thought of the motel's part in Farren's success the more he understood his Aunt Ellen would love it. Family had been important to her and if she knew the Landseer would help new happy families connect, she'd be ecstatic.

Delphine seemed happy with the idea too. Of course, she was happy. She thought her scheme to throw Farren at him had worked. After all, Farren had moved into her room last night. As far as Delphine knew, Farren had moved in with Grady. Into Grady's house. She didn't need to know the real arrangement.

Until last night's move, he hadn't seen Farren since he'd cooked her a burger and shown her the wooden walkway and painted playground equipment. They'd talked and texted about Singles Fest, but otherwise had kept their lives separate.

But last night, as he'd helped her with her furniture, he realized he'd missed seeing her. It was odd because he'd only set eyes on her a handful of times. Each time was a revelation though. She was so different from the women he knew. Down-to-earth and hardworking.

She was unaffected and lovely. Her appeal was feminine strength and determination and he looked forward to getting to know her better. Peeling the layers of Farren back to reveal her soft core. And he knew she was soft inside. Her heart especially. She was willing to give up a year of a personal life to build Singles Fest. In effect, she was giving him the year. Him and his fake dating scam. Not many women he knew would make a sacrifice like that.

Yes, women in New York careers logged long hours, gave up dating, and family time for less reward than their male counterparts. He knew that. He had a sister who reminded him regularly how much less most women were paid. O'Hara paid employees well across the board and didn't demand office staff work weekends and late nights unless they wanted to. But being a global broker meant time zones and some of his agents had to work odd hours. They were compensated very well.

But Farren worked with a dedication to her business he admired, while still having time for herself. He'd seen her from afar as she strolled the beach or had lunch with Eva. Farren's life was well-rounded. Small town.

He understood now why she'd stayed in Last Chance Beach. She understood the value in the place, in the lifestyle. He admired her and the determination to stick with the place despite all the reasons he saw for leaving. The thought surprised him.

THE SUN WAS STILL LOW on the morning horizon, the breeze cool and fresh as Farren stood beside the pool and welcomed the new day with a couple of deep breaths. She mentally skipped through her to-do list and smiled. Everything was in order. Still plenty to do, but nothing was awry, and she had no emergencies to sort.

Her first night at the motel had been perfectly quiet and she'd slept straight through. It was quieter on this end of the island. Since the motel was empty, she hadn't heard any late-night revelers returning home after partying on the beach.

She decided to grab her tablet and sit out by the pool to work. She could wrap up in that pretty peach-colored throw she had draped over her sofa back and spend the next hour out here listening to birds and breathing in the salt air.

Trying not to think about Grady. He'd left without a goodbye. Not that she'd expected one, exactly, but it would've been nice to wave him off. To ask if he'd ever come back. But she'd heard his car drive off as she'd woken, and the chance had been taken from her. Maybe it had been her last chance to talk with him face to face.

She hoped not.

He'd shown up in Last Chance Beach and moved into his great-aunt's place in stealth mode. Grady O'Hara had disappeared from public life, ghosted his sister, and holed up for six months. The man was perfectly capable of ghosting Farren if the mood struck.

She hoped he didn't. She wanted to see him again. He wasn't nearly as grumpy as he'd seemed at first.

Mellow Grady could be kind, funny, and caring. She liked Mellow Grady and imagined that was how he'd been when he'd fallen for his fiancée. Veronica had seen him at his most charming when he'd pursued her.

She wondered if it had been love at first sight between him and Veronica. Some people claimed that happened, but she had major doubts.

The last time she'd seen Grumpy Grady had been when he'd loomed over her at the Sandbar Bar and Grill at the Sands. Had he been jealous of her talking with Archie and Jesse? He'd certainly made it clear they were "seeing" each other.

Not that he'd been possessive. Once he realized what the four of them were discussing, he'd joined in and seemed at ease. And since then, he'd been Mellow Grady, Kind Grady, and most helpful. Sweet, even.

But still, he'd left without a last goodbye. She sighed and turned toward her unit. With her hand on the door, she heard light, hurried footsteps coming around the motel office.

Whoever it was, they were on a mission. With a nervous flutter in her mind, a sense she often listened to, she stepped back from the door.

Delphine barreled around the shadowy corner by the office and into the morning light.

"Delphine! I didn't know you were stopping by. How've you been?" *Don't babble. She can't have seen you with your hand on the doorknob.* She hid the offending hand behind her back and felt a rush of heat to her face. *Stupid light complexion.*

"I thought I'd check to see how things are going with the motel and your plans for Singles Fest." No hello. No *gotcha* glance. Just a breezy smile that belonged on a friend.

Farren smoothed her hair and tucked it behind her ears for something to do.

Delphine was a feminine form of her brother. A solidly built woman with strong shoulders, a straight back, and next-to-no waist. Formidable to say the least. Her eyes were sharper, more critical, than Grady's or maybe that was because Farren felt guilty about lying. It was so much easier on the phone.

She set the guilt aside because, after spending time with Grady, she understood that Delphine had never been her friend, not when she inquired about the business, not when she encouraged Farren to approach Grady and definitely not when she'd pushed her to have that extra glass of wine. To Delphine, Farren was a means to an end.

That end being a brother who was back at work, and in a relationship.

Delphine was a predator, determined to achieve her goal. The fact that Grady's sister felt obligated to fix her brother's life was beside the point. Delphine was relentless.

"Of course, it's nice of you to stop by to see me," Farren responded smoothly. "I was heading to check that the linens are in order. Walk with me? It's too bad you missed Grady by a few minutes." She frowned because Delphine should've known her brother's schedule.

Clearly, she wanted to catch Farren alone. *Hm. What was she up to?*

"I'm dying for coffee. I left the hotel without breakfast." Delphine wore an expectant expression.

The Sands, where Delphine stayed, had coffee machines in all the rooms and a huge urn in the lobby. The idea that Delphine had bypassed it all didn't sit right. Grady's sister wanted inside Grady's house.

For a second Farren panicked, then she remembered that the key to the house was on the ring with all the other motel keys. She'd also been in Grady's kitchen often enough to know where he kept the coffee. "I'll go put on a pot. Would you like to bring it along while we walk?"

"No. I'd like to come inside with you."

"Sure thing." Another flutter of nerves that Farren beat back. She could do this. If she didn't, Grady might pull the plug on their agreement. Then she'd be kicked out of the motel and Singles Fest would flounder before it had a chance.

Like a mouse with a cat breathing down its neck, Farren led the way to the house's private entrance. She held the entire ring of keys hidden in her palm as she used the house key, not that it mattered because Delphine was busy looking into the interior of Farren's car. "It's so tiny in there."

"It's roomy enough for the driver," she responded vaguely as she held the door open for her visitor.

"Grady's never been in it, has he?"

Farren laughed. "Of course not. He's convinced he wouldn't fit." *Nice save.* Grady had never mentioned her car. She followed Delphine inside and flipped on the lights. Grady had left the place tidy. But then, he was a tidy man.

Delphine looked around with interest. "I'm surprised you didn't bring any of your own furniture when you moved in. This place looks exactly the same as when my aunt lived here." She eyed the dead plant in the corner. "She fussed over that Ficus."

"Grady forgot to water it." Farren moved into the kitchen. "I plan to buy a replacement."

"And your furniture?"

"I sublet my place furnished," she lied.

Delphine eyed her. "You kept your apartment?"

Farren shrugged. "Grady and I haven't known each other long," she said with a cool breeze in her voice that said it was not Delphine's business. She made for the kitchen and started the coffee. "And I can use the income."

She bent to search the fridge, dismissing Delphine's line of questions. Great. Grady had left milk inside. Relieved, she pulled it out and set the half-full carton on the table.

Her phone rang and her heart skipped a beat when she saw that it was Grady calling. She gave a silent thank you as she answered. "Hi, sweetheart," she crooned happily.

"She's there," Grady intoned. He was a smart man. She'd liked smart men. "When my sister wasn't at the office or picking up at home, I figured she'd waylaid you."

"Of course," she replied with a smile in her voice. "It's no problem."

"Does she know you moved into the unit?"

"Not at all." She kept her voice a happy singsong. "Your sister's here. We're having coffee."

"Where?"

A question she couldn't see how to answer without giving something away. So she moved the conversation into left field and hoped he'd play along.

"Did I tell you the linens were delivered yesterday? I don't know if I mentioned it." She clasped the phone closely and chuckled in an intimate way. She turned and walked a few steps into the living room. A shared breath, delight in hearing from him, a warm smile on her face and in her tone. The type of conversation any newly minted couple would have, she hoped.

"You deserve an acting award," he said in his deep gravel voice. Thrills chased down her spine at the approval.

"I know, right? I'm about to check the linen but I don't anticipate a problem. And I'll be interviewing people to staff the motel later today. From now on linen will be someone else's responsibility." This last part was the bald truth. The motel details bogged her down and she'd be thrilled to pass them along to an employee.

"Can you handle interviews on your own? Have you ever done them?"

For a second, she wanted to admit she dreaded them. But he didn't need to hear that. Grady had his own problems and wouldn't want to hear about her nerves. "I'll be fine," she said. "I've done a few." But final decisions had belonged to higher-ups.

"Get Delphine to help," he said firmly. Part of her wanted to protest that she could do it herself, but she'd be foolish to pass up a chance to learn. "It's the least she can do," he continued, "after springing this neat little trap. She's only there to see if you've really moved in."

"Yes, you're right, sweetheart. It's all going smoothly," she assured him, continuing with her happy girlfriend charade.

"Still, *honeybunch*," he said, sounding delighted, "you should pick her brain about interviewing people. She's done it for years."

"Will do. Thanks for the tip." She tried for a seductive chuckle but wasn't sure she pulled it off. Delphine was looking through Grady's kitchen cupboards, distracting her.

"Okay," Grady said briskly, and she felt his dismissal. She heard horns honking and the sounds of traffic. "I'm heading into the airport. I'll call tonight."

"Really?" She blurted, surprised that he'd offer to talk again so soon. Until now, when they'd been busy, they hadn't made time for each other. "I'll look forward to it," she promised, like a lovestruck teen.

Her cheeks warming, she disconnected and turned to face Delphine. She was pouring coffee for them both. She held up a mug. "Shall we go look at towels and sheets?"

THE RELATIVELY SHORT flight to JFK went without a hitch. All the while he only had half his mind on his laptop. The other half filled with concern about Farren being stuck with his sister, as she lied to cover up the truth of their relationship. Delphine was a bloodhound.

Still, he didn't want to call the game. He was having fun helping Farren, seeing her dreams come to fruition. Painting the playground equipment and rebuilding the walkway had been therapeutic and he felt better than he had in years.

Better than he had with Veronica in the early days. He should feel a pang of guilt for that, but he didn't.

It wasn't until Grady walked into the lobby of his condo building that he realized everything Veronica had left behind would still be in his home. The realization drove all his warm thoughts of Farren from his mind.

He walked to the security desk and Albert's face lit up at the sight of him. "Mr. O'Hara, you're back." His smile dimmed as he remembered what had driven Grady away in the first place. "I want to offer my condolences, sir."

"Thanks, Albert," he said with a deep sigh. "I'm going to need some help with boxes and clothes."

Albert held up a hand to stop him. "Of course, whatever you need. I saved all the cards from the floral arrangements that arrived in the days after." He reached into a drawer at the bottom of his desk. The stack of envelopes was thick and ranged from bright pink to somber charcoal. "I think some of these were for the wedding and the rest..."

"I'll take them all. Thanks." He'd hand them off to Delphine and she could decide how to handle the wedding wishes and the condolences. He assumed some were from the same people, sent days apart. "Would you mind coming up with me? I'll wait if you need to get someone to cover the desk."

"I'm off shift in a few minutes, so as soon as Felicia arrives, I'd be happy to help."

Fifteen minutes later, Grady opened his door and walked into his apartment with Albert. Gaily wrapped packages sat just inside the door in three stacks. Wedding gifts Veronica had let known she wanted. Grady had no idea what she'd asked for.

But he knew enough to keep the cards with the gifts so Delphine could return everything. She wouldn't mind. "I should have seen to all this before now." He frowned.

"No, Mr. O'Hara," Albert said with a sad shake of his head. "Nobody would expect you to handle this on top of everything else. I'm sure Ms. O'Hara will help, and your friends will understand."

"I haven't been the nicest guy lately, Albert. I've spent a lot of time ignoring my sister." He shrugged out of his jacket and tossed it over a chair in the living room. The chair was soft pink and had fancy legs and satin upholstery. Veronica's choice, not his. "Wanna beer? There should still be a couple in the fridge. It couldn't have gone skunky yet, right?"

"Right, should be fine. But I shouldn't, Mr. O'Hara. Drinking on the job can get me fired." Albert shifted. "I took the liberty of coming in and emptying your fridge of anything that could go bad. When you told me not to let anyone else in, I didn't want you coming home to a big mess in there."

"I appreciate that. I didn't expect to be away this long, but time got away from me."

Alberta nodded, his eyes sad and understanding. He clasped his hands together and looked prepared to wait.

"I'll go look in the bedroom, see what I have to deal with in there, hm?"

When he walked in, he saw an explosion of clothing. Veronica had been half-unpacked. On the bed were winter jackets and coats, sweaters, a heavy robe for wintry nights and woolly socks in piles. In the closet she'd hung her lightweight clothes; sundresses and silky tops filled her side of the walk-in. Sandals in all colors lined the floor. He remembered then that she'd planned to have the closet organizer come after the honeymoon. A professional, she'd said, would whip this small space into shape and give her the room she deserved.

He walked through the nine-foot-long closet, running a finger along the row of dresses, making them shift and sway on their hangers. He wanted to feel more than relief, but he couldn't dredge up anything close to sorrow. He'd done all that and left it behind when he'd learned Veronica had drowned on the way to meet her lover.

The night before she was to marry Grady, she'd hopped into a canoe with three glasses of champagne in her belly and no life vest on. She'd paddled out into the lake to cross to a rental cabin. She'd hit something floating in the water. At least that was the theory. A branch, maybe.

While he'd been shooting the breeze with his best man and college buddies, his bride had sunk beneath the still waters of the lake. The tradition of not seeing the bride after midnight had given her the chance to escape the celebrations.

He'd spent weeks wondering what would possess her to go out in a canoe alone. He'd blamed himself for not noticing that she was having second thoughts or wedding jitters. But it wasn't anything like that.

Their two-year relationship had been a fraud. That was the only way he could think of it. She'd been with this other guy since before she'd become his assistant. Delphine had hired Veronica and his sister had seen the perfect woman for her busy brother.

Back in the bedroom he spied a jewelry box on the dresser. He opened it and fingered through a collection of rings, bracelets, and earrings. He'd have to call Veronica's mother to warn her he'd be sending them. Something like this shouldn't arrive out of the blue.

By the time he returned to the living room, Albert had poured him a beer in a pilsner glass, the foam head perfect. "I was a bartender in another life," he said with a coaxing smile. "Rough in there?"

"Rough, yeah. Thanks," he said as he took the glass. "Feel free to help yourself if you want one."

He nodded. "I'm off the clock now. I'll head downstairs and come up with a moving dolly for these gifts so I can store them for you. I'll bring back some empty boxes for whatever you found in there?"

"No, it's fine. She still had the boxes her clothes came out of in the corner of the room. We can use those. If you've got time." He blew out a breath. "I can do this myself if you have to get home."

Albert shook his head. "No problem. I've already called my wife. I'll be right back and when we're done, I'll have that beer. The wife said she'd come by too if you need her."

"How is Sha'Shauna? Good?"

"Pregnant with number three. She's in that weepy stage, so if you need her to help, be warned."

Grady smiled and nodded. "Thanks, but you and I will manage." He wasn't sure what the weepy stage was, but he didn't feel like seeing it firsthand. "While you're gone, I'll make a couple of calls. I need to talk with Veronica's mother and my sister. They can sort out what to do about the gifts and her clothes." He wondered where all the expensive jewelry he'd given her as gifts had ended up because none of it had been in the box on the dresser.

"Women are stronger about these things. At least, the women I know are. You're sure you don't want Sha'Shauna to come over?"

"We both know how to hang dresses and fold sweaters. And I don't know that I want to see your wife in tears." And going through a dead woman's clothes might trigger a flood from Albert's wife. He'd met Sha'Shauna a couple of times, and she seemed an empathetic, warm-hearted woman. He wouldn't want to upset her.

"Gotcha. You're right." Albert gave him a pat on the shoulder. "We can do this." Albert left to get the dolly.

He shouldn't hand off the work involved in these arrangements to Delphine and Veronica's mom, but Albert was right. If left to Grady, the gifts and clothes would sit in the lobby storage room forever. Out of sight, out of mind. And Delphine didn't need anything else to pester him about.

Unreturned wedding gifts would stick in her mind, and she'd never give him a minute's rest.

He wondered how Farren was managing and reached for the phone to call her but stayed his hand. He needed to focus on his task. Albert had stayed late to help him and, as difficult as this next hour would be, he had to face it.

Chapter Twelve

TEN P.M.

Farren decided Grady wasn't calling. His promise to talk tonight had only been a reaction to their fake phone call silliness. She shouldn't have put any stock in it.

She'd had a stress-filled day with Delphine. Every word Farren said had had to be weighed against the desire to be honest. But Grady was adamant about not wanting Delphine sticking her nose into his life. Farren had respected his wishes.

After spending the day with his sister, Farren couldn't blame Grady for guarding his privacy.

The more time she'd spent with Delphine, the more she could see how he would need to distance himself from her controlling behavior. The towels hadn't been stacked to her satisfaction and some of the sheets were a different shade of white. White was white to Farren and while she agreed about the slight difference in hue, it didn't matter to her, nor would it matter to guests.

She and Delphine had spent over an hour matching the hues for the top and bottom sheets. Apparently, it wouldn't do to have a cool white on the bottom and a warmer white on top. Delphine had wanted the sheets paired with the same color hue to prevent mixing the shades.

Finally, Farren had snapped. "The only person in the entire world who'd notice this slight difference, *at a budget motel*, would be you."

Delphine had *hmphed* in her throat. "Or someone else who cares what they're sleeping on."

Farren had slumped against the stack of towels. "If they care that much, they wouldn't be a guest of the Landseer, would they?"

Something about the purse of Delphine's lips said Farren's outburst had been satisfying. Odd thing to see.

Since Grady had decided not to call, she decided a bath would help her decompress before bed. She could read a bit and soak until she felt relaxed for sleep. She added lavender scented bath salts to the water and let the steam rise while she undressed in the bedroom. Her robe already hung from the hook behind the bathroom door, so she dropped her clothes, grabbed her phone from the arm of her sofa and returned to the bathroom. There, she drew in several deep breaths while she set the phone on the floor beside the tub. She turned off the faucet, stepped into the tub and then sank into the water.

The bath enclosure had been recovered and shone like new. The tub wasn't deep, but she'd manage by sliding down until her shoulders were covered. Later, she'd scooch up, so her legs got the benefit of the soak.

She leaned over the tub wall and checked her messages for anything important, sighed when she realized she was free for the rest of the night, and sank into the water to just below her nose. The lavender scent soothed, and the hot water eased her shoulder and neck muscles. She wasn't sore, exactly, but tired from the stress of the day and Delphine. The woman was draining.

Someday, she mused, she'd have a deep soaker tub of her own and love every decadent moment using it.

Her phone buzzed and she startled. Peering over the rim of the tub, she saw Grady's name on the screen. She flicked her fingers to get as much water off them as possible while the phone buzzed insistently. She wiped her hands across the terry floor mat and hit the answer button where the phone lay.

"Hi," she called. "Hold on, I'm wet." She dragged the floor mat up and dried both hands completely before picking up the phone. So much for her quiet soak. Still, she felt warmth flow through her, and not from the hot water.

"Are you in the tub?" Grady asked, his voice at least an octave lower than usual.

Oh, she really didn't want him imagining her. Did she?

"No, I'm ah...washing dishes."

He chuckled in her ear. "Sure, you are. Because that's what everyone does at ten thirty at night. You forget that I know what an accomplished liar you are."

"You wouldn't say that if you saw the blush in my cheeks. I give myself away."

His chuckle deepened as it resonated through her. Her body responded in ways that would've shocked her younger self.

"I'm sorry for calling this late," he said. "I tried to finish up earlier, but once word was out that I was here, the texts and calls wouldn't stop. I've been hounded into my foxhole."

He sounded tired and she made a sympathetic sound in her throat.

"I'm not used to this anymore," he went on. "When I was in Last Chance Beach, people respected my privacy and kept their messages and calls to emergencies only. Also, last time I was here, I had an assistant to screen calls and handle the small stuff." He hitched a breath and paused. "But I'm done talking about my day. How was yours?"

The poor man must have been reminded at every turn that Veronica wasn't with him now. He had no assistant and no bride. She kept her tone light because he'd been surrounded by darkness all day.

"Poor you." She crooned. "I sympathize. It's hard being the boss. When I worked at the Sands, I was part of a team but now? Wow, all the decisions are mine." It was a challenge.

"If you win you get the credit but if you fail you can't blame anyone but yourself."

"And for you, there's the added concern about keeping people employed." He had offices in New York and other large cities across the globe.

"I keep the operation as small as I can. Some of my people work from home in other markets."

"Oh, I wasn't sure." She'd been picturing private jets and yachts and all the trappings of billionaires at play.

"We keep big business happy, Farren. But we're not huge ourselves. We find whatever real estate holdings our clients need. Factories in the Midwest. Or land for housing developments. Or repurposing malls that have closed. It's a tough, competitive business that runs on networking and connections. My time away was noted."

She sank to shoulder height in the water, which meant her wet knees were exposed.

"When I have my own place, I'm installing a really deep tub," she muttered. If Singles Fest was the success she dreamed it could be, she had her eye on a cottage down the beach. Nearly derelict, it sat alone and—

"I'm trying not to think of you in the tub," Grady murmured in her ear, "so I'd appreciate it if you skipped the commentary so I can continue not thinking of you wet in the tub." He cleared his throat. "Did you fake out Delphine?"

She splashed to a full sit, trying to dispel the thought of him imagining her nude.

"Your splashing isn't helping, Farren."

"Sorry, I'll try to keep still. Do you still want to talk?"

There was a long pause.

And then, he responded, still raspy, still deep. "How did things go with my sister?"

With an inward sigh of relief, she spoke in a subdued tone. "She can be hard to read sometimes. But, yes, I believe she believes we're dating." She wished he'd let the whole being in the bathtub thing go. It was too intimate for their relationship.

If they were really dating, they could have some fun with the situation, but they weren't dating and they weren't intimate, no matter how sexy and alluring his deep voice sounded in her ear.

She told him about the discussion with Delphine in the linen supply closet. "It was a total waste of time, but she was so set on sorting the sheets her way."

"She's a perfectionist, but this seems too much, even for her. She was testing you."

"I can't say why I went along with her." She huffed. "One minute I had lots of other things to do and the next she had me holding the cool toned white sheets while she dug out the warmer hued sheets. We paired cool with cool and warm with warm. I'm still not sure why I allowed it." She'd left a few other small jobs undone because Delphine had wasted so much time.

"I'm nodding my head in case you're wondering," he said with a quiet chuckle. "But I can't explain her motives. She's not *your* sister, so I don't understand why she'd interfere with you or your day. You handled the visit to the house okay, right?"

"Yes, I know where you keep your coffee, and we didn't linger in there. She did note that I hadn't brought any of my furniture to your place."

She hadn't conjured a visual of Grady until now, but the thought came to her that he could be stretched out on his bed as they talked. She squeezed her eyes shut to dispel the image, but no luck. Was he under the covers or on top? Dressed or in his boxers ready to sleep? Or maybe he wore briefs.

Or nothing at all.

She gulped.

"I think I understand why you've avoided her lately." She didn't agree with sibling estrangements but sometimes a break could be a good thing.

"I have my reasons," he said gravely. "Did you get through your interviews?"

"Yes, and Delphine was a great help. I learned a lot. It's tough knowing someone is sitting in front of you who really needs the job, and you only have a limited number to go around. Fifteen people showed up for each position."

She'd given priority to the previous employees, but some of them were aging out of the workforce. "A few of the old-timers who worked for your great-aunt should be retired, but I didn't have the heart to pass them over."

"Maybe they came in out of curiosity."

"Maybe. But I appreciated Delphine being there. She kept me on track and was kind to everyone without giving away her opinion."

"Which she shared with you as soon as each interview was over, right?"

"Right. I took lots of notes."

He chuckled and the sound reverberated down to her wet, lavender-scented toes.

"I'm sure you did," he said quietly, as if he knew the effect he was having. She almost forgot what they were talking about.

"I'll call the people I'm hiring in the morning and once they've said yes or no, I'll advise the others by email or text, if they prefer." Delphine had said most employers don't contact the people they decide not to hire, but Farren felt that was rude. People showed up for a job and they deserved the courtesy of knowing the outcome.

"Good. Last Chance Beach is a small town and word gets around if you're not a good employer and courtesy is appreciated." He paused. "How are things otherwise?"

"Fine. Everything's fine." She smiled and she knew he'd hear it in her next words. "What about you? I want to know all the details about your triumphant return to the Big Apple. I know you must have been reminded of Veronica, and I'm sorry for that. But did you realize you miss the city? Or did you have a different reaction?"

"It's a pain. Too many people want too much of my time, and I'm already tired of the hustle. It's crowded and loud and when I was younger, I loved it. The clubs and parties, the way business runs; everything was fun. But now? These last few months have changed me."

"Oh. Well, loss will do that. It's normal." She shouldn't have asked.

"I wanted to call earlier, but I needed to talk with some people about Veronica's clothes and personal things. I don't keep my phone by the bed and you're my last call of the day."

"Oh." Was she an afterthought or the last item on an exhausting must-do list?

"I saved the best for last," he admitted softly. His voice traveled the length of her this time, warming her and making her feel too much.

"That's nice of you to say. I admit I looked forward to chatting tonight. It's different knowing you're not in town. We don't see each other much, but it seems odd that I can't knock on your door and chat."

"Do you want to?" His voice lowered even more. "Knock on my door to talk?"

She shifted and winced when she realized he must hear the water slosh with every movement.

"Sometimes." The bath was beginning to chill, but she couldn't stand up because he'd know. He'd already taken a mental picture of her; she didn't need to add to the portfolio. "Yes," she admitted. "Especially at the end of the day, like this. It would be great to have someone to bounce ideas around with."

"I'd like that, too. There's something about clearing your mind when the rush of the day is over."

She heard a rustle in the background. It was faint, but real. "Are you in the living room?"

"No."

The rustle she heard meant he could only be in one other place. *Oh.* "But you said you don't keep your phone by the bed anymore."

"I didn't say I was in bed, Farren."

"Okay." Whatever the rustle was, it was none of her business. She mentally erased the image of him stretched out on rumpled sheets. Well, she tried to, anyway. Once she conjured the scene, it was impossible to get rid of.

He sighed loudly and she imagined his hot breath in her ear. Oh, she had it bad. Now she was having auditory fantasies on top of the visuals she was trying hard to wipe.

"I should go," he said, with reluctance. "I've got an early start tomorrow."

She didn't want to hang up, but this had to end sometime. "I'm turning into a prune anyway."

"Can we do this again tomorrow night?"

"I'll be around," she said coolly, as if it didn't matter if he called or not.

"Then it's a date." He chuckled as he disconnected.

GRADY ROSE FROM THE bed, shucked his jockeys, and tossed them in his laundry basket. No way could he tell Farren he'd been stretched out, thinking of her in that too-shallow bathtub, naked. He hadn't even tried to get the images out his mind. Truth was, he didn't want to because he was curious about her. He'd nuzzled her neck, bussed her cheek, held her hand, cooked for her and laughed with her. Their kisses had been far too chaste, and he wasn't sure when he'd decided that had to change.

He had a lot to look forward to and it had been a long time since he'd felt this way.

He padded out to the kitchen, put his phone on the counter, mentally thanked Veronica for insisting on the distance between his bed and the phone and then wandered back to bed. Sleep would take a long time to come tonight.

Chapter Thirteen

JULY 3 THE LANDSEER Motel

Farren stood by the pool behind a table with brochures and a schedule to hand out to each family group as they arrived. Her stomach was rolling and bounding like an Olympic gymnast from one side of her body to the other. She'd been taking deep breaths since she'd woken up, trying to contain her nerves. She told herself they helped. "Welcome to Singles Fest, I'm Farren Parks, your host."

She shook hands with an excited redhead with the classic light blue eyes and creamy white skin. A bridge of freckles decorated her nose. But her smile made her whole body look as if it were lit from the inside. "I'm Val Andrews and this is my son, Topher."

Val looked to be in her early thirties and eager for a good time. Exactly the type of client Singles Fest aimed for. Farren handed her the brochure for Barnacle Bill's Minigolf and the menu from the J Roger. Thanks to Grady's phone call to Bill Fester, grandson Tom saw the wisdom of helping a new business that was trying to increase tourism for the whole community.

She tapped the brochure to draw Val's eye. "You'll find a discount coupon if you want to go play separately from the group outing. And the J Roger restaurant is a nice stroll's distance along the beach. But we're having a welcome barbecue with hot dogs and burgers at five-thirty, right here."

"This will be so much fun," Val replied as she looked at the papers in her hand. "It's lovely to meet you." She squeezed Topher's hand. "We're going to have a blast."

Topher nodded his head at his mother. Then he looked at Farren. "Hullo, nice to meetcha."

"I hope you have a lot of fun," Farren said to the boy. She leaned toward Val to share her secret. "This is the first weekend for Singles Fest and if you need anything or have any suggestions on how to make this more fun, I'm listening."

"Just having Topher entertained while I'm out with real live grownups sounds wonderful." The woman said with a shy smile. "That's why I'm here, so we can have a break from each other, and both have fun on our own. And have fun together, too."

Topher, who looked about seven, chimed in. "I want to learn to swim," he said with a look of longing at the pool.

Farren hadn't arranged for lessons. An oversight, but a great idea.

"I'm sorry, but we don't have swimming lessons on the schedule." At his disappointed look, she went on, "But I'll see if I can arrange something for you Topher." She scrambled mentally. Maybe she could beg Eva for a favor this one time.

"We do have a lifeguard for the organized pool time," she assured Val. "I love the idea of offering lessons." She grinned at Topher. "Thanks for asking about them."

"We'll manage," Val said happily. "I can get him into the shallow end and see if he floats," she teased. "But he may be too full of candy and fast food." It was Val's turn to lean in over the table. "He's already been having treats in the car. The drive from Richmond was fun. Just the two of us, no phones, no work, and all the anticipation of the weekend."

Clearly, Val was her perfect client. Here for fun with her child, but also needing a break from single parenting. And maybe there'd be a special connection with someone. Farren's heart filled with happy anticipation for Val and Topher.

She directed the small family to their room and looked up for the next person in line.

"Grady!"

"Hi, there. I'll pass on the brochures." He held up his hand and she let Barnacle Bill's brochure flutter to the table.

"What are you doing here? You said next week sometime." He'd been gone for a month, and he'd become vague about ever coming home, so this was a real surprise. They'd talked every day since that first time. She'd come to look forward to the flirty chats, although she'd made sure to never be wet and naked since that first time. He made time to call her at the end of her day, no matter what time zone he was in.

Last night he'd been in New York and their chat had been rushed because they'd both worked late, and she'd been tired and too wired to relax. She'd promised to be more interesting tonight, assuming she'd have a lot to share about the guests.

And now, here he stood. His face looked dear and sweet and not grumpy at all. It was hard not to round the table and give him a hug. She might not want to let go. Looking not grouchy wasn't the only difference in Grady. His jaw looked shadowed rather than sharp, stubbled rather than smooth. "You're growing a beard?"

He scrubbed a palm across his chin, and she wanted to do the same thing.

"You like it?" he asked, looking surprised. "I didn't take time to shave the last couple of days."

"Depends. Are you going bushman again?" She teased and cocked her head.

He ducked his head in a way that made her heart roll over and showed her the boy he'd once been. "No, I got bored and too busy and when it grew in a bit, I thought I'd go to the barber here. I liked the guy. He can give me a look that suits my face. I'd make an uneven mess."

A sexy, tidy beard. Nice. "You'll look very handsome."

"You think?"

"I said so, didn't I? Have I ever lied to you?"

A cloud crossed his features. "Not that I'm aware of."

That meant an important someone had lied to him before. She couldn't imagine who, aside from Delphine, but she didn't seem like an outright liar. No, she was more of a benevolent manipulator. Her heart was in the right place; she just wasn't normally upfront about her agenda.

She decided to ignore his odd comment. Not that she wasn't curious, but this wasn't the time or place to quiz him on faithless people in his life. "You didn't answer me. Why are you here so early?"

"I wouldn't miss the launch. No way." He hooked a thumb over his shoulder. "There's a line up to check in at the office. You'll be inundated in a minute. But swing by the house when the crowd dies down. Later tonight, when you're done, we can sit on the beach and talk there instead of on the phone."

A wave of delight washed over her heart. "Great idea." She couldn't say anything more because he was right. There were at least two families heading her way.

GRADY HAD NEEDED TO see Farren's smile, feel her freshness and honesty so he'd blown off his in-person meetings for the day and rushed to the airport. He could do his staff evaluations by video chat instead. He planned on groveling and thanking everyone profusely anyway. Not one of them had let him down while he'd holed up at the Landseer. Every staff member had stepped up in support and he'd already arranged special bonuses for all of them.

Only hours later, he stood here in front of Farren, drinking in the sight of her. In the flesh. He'd missed her every day he'd been in New York. They hadn't video chatted this last month, mostly because he loved the sound of her breathy, quiet voice in his ear late at night. She'd never asked to "see" him online, either. The phone seemed more intimate somehow. Quieter, softer.

Sexier.

A little kid rushed the table, staring at the brochures and exclaiming happily. "Look at this one!"

"Later then," Grady said to Farren. She looked so happy, bursting with pride and excitement. Later, he'd feed off it and cheer her on. After all, that's why he'd come home.

Home. The word had a ring to it.

"I'm looking forward to it," she said with a long look into his eyes. She gave him a small wave as he stepped away so the next family could get their welcome package.

He strolled through the gathering people toward his private entrance. Kids squealed behind him accompanied by the sounds of shushing parents and laughter. He'd been dead set against hearing the happy sounds when she'd first put forth her proposition.

But now? His rusty heart lightened at the joy he heard all around him. He smiled to himself as he fit his key into the lock and turned it.

Singles Fest. Who'd have thought there were so many single parents looking for partners? Farren had been right, though. The successful people he knew had no problem finding their next spouse, it was keeping them that was the problem.

As he turned to close the door, a man's voice called Farren's name in a happy tone. Curious, Grady held the door open to see who had called to her.

"Denny! What a surprise. How are you?" Farren's response was warm and kind as she looked up into the man's face.

Denny stepped around the table, wrapped her in his arms and spun her in a circle. She laughed at the manhandling.

Grady narrowed his eyes. His grip tightened on the handle of his leather bag. The boy who'd rushed the table belonged to this guy. And it seemed like he had two other younger kids with him, too. A single father of three who knew Farren well enough to hug her had come for Singles Fest. Not only did he know Farren, but this Denny looked deep into her eyes and made her smile. The tilt of her head and the joy in her face was telling.

They'd had a thing once. Was he one of the men she'd dated for a couple of weeks? A tourist returned. Or did their connection go back further?

Where did this guy know Farren from?

As much as he wanted to study their reunion for more clues, he didn't. Standing here gawking while his fake girlfriend chatted with a long-lost somebody from her past was beneath him.

But he wanted to gawk. No, scratch that. He wanted to walk over there and pull Farren into his arms for a welcome home kiss and let this Romeo see what was what.

Farren wouldn't appreciate it, though. And he'd far outgrown the Neanderthal most men had lurking inside. She'd agreed to stop by the house later and they had a date to hit the beach. He felt sure she'd tell him everything then.

He had fires to put out in New York and they needed his attention. Also, it wasn't fair to keep his employees waiting any longer for their reviews.

Aside from the reviews, he'd blown off several meetings. He tossed his bag to the floor and made his first call. To Delphine.

"Are you in Last Chance Beach?" he asked by way of greeting. She'd left the office early yesterday and he'd assumed she was coming here. Not that they'd chatted about anything other than work. He'd kept her at arm's length for the whole time he'd been in New York. No personal chat. No questions answered unless they pertained to the running of O'Hara Enterprises. She balked at first, but she'd had no choice but to accept his boundaries.

"Of course I'm here, aren't you?" She sniped back.

"Yes."

"Good. You should be. You abandoned your new girlfriend for a month right after she moved in with you." And this was why he'd avoided talking about Farren while they were at work. The woman was enough of a distraction during the day.

He'd saved his favorite distraction for their nightly chats. Like a sweet treat he craved before sleep.

He blinked. Delphine was right, it did *look* as if he'd abandoned his girlfriend after she moved in. But Farren knew the truth and that's what mattered.

He'd almost forgotten the fake part of this thing with Farren because his feelings had become real during their late-night phone calls. It had happened gradually, sneakily, without him noticing. Could he trust himself in this? Trust *her*?

He'd made a bad call with Veronica. But that didn't mean Farren was the same kind of woman. Even if that Denny guy looked ready to kiss her and she'd given him her very best smile.

Ignoring Delphine's jibe, he changed the subject. "I delivered Veronica's jewelry box to her parents yesterday." It was a bald statement of fact but guaranteed to get his sister's mind off Farren.

"How were they? I saw them at the funeral."

"Yeah, that's still a blur to me. And to them. But they're devastated. Glad to see me, though." Guilt rose at the way he'd played along as the grieving partner. They'd had no idea their daughter had been cheating on him all through their time together. Veronica had had another man when they'd started dating, when Grady had proposed, and as she and her mother had planned the wedding.

They'd never hear the truth from him. They were good people and never needed to know the things he knew about their daughter. Veronica had been their oldest, their shining star who set an example for her two younger sisters.

The only reason he could see for Veronica's actions was greed. She'd planned to divorce him as soon as she could. They'd had no pre-nuptial agreement because he felt he knew her so well after working together day and night. She'd been dedicated, available at all hours, hardworking and committed to his success. They'd planned a future running the company together.

As he recalled it, she'd mentioned a pre-nuptial agreement once and he'd been the one to say it wasn't necessary. The fact that her question had been asked during post-coital glow made him shake his head now.

He'd been a fool.

"Will I see you this trip?" His sister's question brought him back to the conversation. Her tone was hesitant, as if she were afraid of the answer.

One of the reasons he'd avoided being alone with her was so she couldn't press him for details about Farren, or Veronica.

He didn't want to tell Delphine the truth about Veronica, he didn't want to tell anyone. But this estrangement had been hard on her. She came across as pushy, demanding, and selfish, but Delphine loved her family and him especially. She'd handled a lot during his time away from the office. She deserved to know why he'd gone silent. It was time to clear the air.

"Yes, we'll see each other. It's time to talk."

DENNIS BRACKEN HADN'T changed since high school. He still had his rakish good looks, still had a smile that pulled at her heartstrings and his eyes still glowed with mischief. The fact that his mischief had brought mayhem to two women's lives disturbed her. A lot.

Denny wanted to kiss her. The urge was plain. It was in his eyes, and in the way he'd swept her up into a hug and in the way he'd angled his face. She dodged the kiss and gave him a smile instead.

He'd had a knack for making her feel like she was the only woman he saw. The only woman in the room. And right now, she was the one in his arms, standing too close.

She wondered if he'd made his wives feel the same. Maybe that's why he'd been able to get away for years with having two families. Too bad one of them had got suspicious and hired a private detective.

Now, he had no one. She knew his family and they'd been devastated. First, learning they had grandchildren they didn't know and secondly that their golden boy had behaved so badly.

Denny's mess had swept through Last Chance Beach like a tidal wave. She knew the light in her eyes dimmed a bit as the knowledge of all he'd done crowded out her delight in seeing him again after all this time. Denny reacted with a sad, slow blink.

Then he smiled and gave her one more squeeze. "You've heard," he said softly.

"Of course." She pulled away from him and cleared her throat. All the things she wanted to say bottled up in her throat, long enough to make her realize he'd probably heard them all. The shock, disdain, disgust at his behavior. She swallowed it all because he was here with his children.

He reached for the handle of a stroller and rolled it back and forth.

"I'm so glad to see you, Farren. You have no idea how much I need a friendly face." He bit his lower lip and looked at her from under his brows. "When I saw your posts about this weekend, I jumped at the chance to get away from all the craziness and bring my kids here."

"How many did you bring?" She was going to meet the poor, confused children. She braced herself and hoped he didn't have any more stashed away.

"Three. This is a getting-to-know-you weekend for them." He tossed his children a glance as they looked at the table and then at their father. A little girl in the stroller had her thumb in her mouth and watched her with happy blue eyes. She was so young to be in the middle of this strange situation. Farren hoped the child was too young to remember the details of her father's deceit.

At the table stood the first boy, who looked to be the oldest, another with auburn hair that didn't come from Denny. His daughter looked younger than two and had bright red ringlets. An angel on earth.

Farren glanced at Denny and saw a multitude of emotions in his eyes. Love, pride, shame trooped across his face and Farren's heart felt the pull of sympathy.

"Oh, you've been busy," she said. His children were beautiful. The older boy held himself stiffly and the shoulder next to the younger boy was turned away. A classic cold shoulder. "And you have your work cut out for you with them," she said under her breath.

"I've landed in a huge mess." Denny's gaze clouded. "But I've had a revelation in all this. And that is, I have to put my kids first from here on in. No more selfish behavior. No more cowardice or taking the easy way."

"Okay." She set aside her judgement as best she could. "I agree they must come first. I'm glad you're here, Denny. We have programs set up for single parents and their children to make new friends. Let's hope it's enough to help your children bond with each other."

"It'll be a start. They're young and I hope they'll adapt." Earnest and open, Denny swept his gaze down her body. "I'm not here for the women. I'm here for them." He looked at the children and nodded at them. The auburn-haired boy gave him a tentative smile.

"Forgive me, but do their mothers know they're here?" she asked.

"Sort of. It's my weekend to have my kids. We've all agreed to that much. Whether I'm at home or here, they're with me." He shrugged.

A line up was forming at the table. "I need to get back to it," she said. "We'll talk later, after things quiet down."

"Sarah goes down for a nap around four. Then to bed right after dinner. In between, she tears around and gets a bit fussy." He smiled affectionately at his daughter.

Denny loved his children like any other father. And kudos to him for bringing them for the weekend by himself. She didn't ask if he'd take them to see his parents in Summerville. That was too personal, too fraught with raw emotion. She supposed Denny wanted to handle things in his own time.

"I'll stop by your room when she's napping. We'll sit outside the door and talk." She gave him the brochures and each child a sucker. The older boy, who reminded her strongly of Denny at ten, asked for a second one for later. Maybe he needed to feel more important or more loved, she didn't know, but she made a show of giving extra suckers to their dad for safekeeping.

After that, the day was a blur, and focus hard to come by. First, she'd been thrilled to see Grady and wanted to spend her day with him, talking and hanging out. She'd missed strolling the beach with him. She missed his grilled burgers.

But she'd see him tonight when the moon was high and the ocean quiet and her guests had all settled in.

There was a welcome barbecue that started at five thirty to accommodate children's bedtimes. After that was over, she'd sit with Denny for a short conversation and then she'd have the rest of the evening to visit with Grady.

She looked forward to it and her heart skipped a beat or two whenever she thought of him.

She couldn't ignore that Denny Bracken had shown up.

Denny had created a landmine field for his children. They were half-siblings and until recently, they'd had their respective mom and a daddy who showed up when he could.

She snagged a coffee from the urn by the pool and hoped it would hold her until she could slip into her room for a quick bite. She'd made sandwiches to last a couple of days because she wouldn't have time for anything more until she hit her stride with the launch.

She sipped the caffeine hit slowly and handled the last of the early arrivals. At noon Eva would be here to lifeguard and the pool would open. That's when she planned to eat her sandwich in peace.

She considered taking her lunch over to Grady's place, but they'd have next-to-no time to talk, and she didn't want to interrupt his workday.

Children began to arrive in bathing suits and sunhats. The distinct scent of sunscreen filled the air and their voices rose in delight.

Eva showed up ten minutes early and Farren unlocked her room so her friend could stow her belongings. "Have you eaten?" she asked.

"Yes, and I brought snacks and water. I've slathered up with sunscreen so I'm good to go."

"We've already had a special request for swimming lessons. I didn't think of offering them, but it makes sense."

Eva nodded. "I'll see what I can do. I know a reliable kid who's certified, but they work on the mainland. Maybe we can set something up for tomorrow or the next day?"

"Great. We'll try but don't worry if it doesn't work out. I didn't make any promises."

With that agreement, Eva stepped outside and Farren had a few moments to herself to think while she ate.

Rumor had it that Denny was in the midst of divorce proceedings from his first wife and a battle for child support and visitation with his common-law wife. If what he'd said was true about this weekend being his time with his children, then at least both women had agreed to weekend visits. She wondered if the women would approve of him being here and introducing the children to each other on his own. She shrugged and decided there was likely no easy way to do any of this.

Being here for the weekend meant the children would have activities, especially the boys. Maybe they'd find a way to be friends.

Maybe they'd land in a tumble of flying fists and kicking feet. Only time would tell, and they had a lifetime to sort out their differences.

What a mess. Denny Bracken was the last person she'd expect to get himself into such a tangle. She wanted to call him every awful name she could think of, but her memories of him intruded, insisting that the young man she remembered would never intentionally plan to ruin two good women and three lovely children.

Chapter Fourteen

FARREN FINISHED HER lunch, stepped out the door of her unit and came face-to-face with Delphine.

"Hi," she said in a weak tone as she quickly pulled the door shut behind her. She smiled when she heard the click at her back. "I didn't know you were in town."

"I wouldn't miss the launch of Singles Fest," Delphine purred. "Not when my brother's here, too." She glanced at the room number on the door. "Whose room is this?"

"It's a break room for me and the other employees," Farren replied as she strode past Grady's sister and headed for the pool. "The lifeguard is a friend of mine, and she also handles daycare and arranges for babysitters if people want to have a private date. She needs a place to hide or eat or check email. I just had a sandwich." *Quit babbling. Delphine knows all this about Eva already. And don't admit to eating anywhere but in Grady's home.*

Farren smiled uneasily until she came up with something nice to say. "Thanks for coming. I don't know that we'd be here at the Landseer without you prodding me to talk to Grady." Which was one hundred percent true.

Delphine surprised her with a hug. "My brother would still be a hermit if you hadn't got him out of the house. I'm going to see him right now." She looked shy at the admission. "He invited me over. Thank you."

"I can't take credit for that. He was probably ready to see you anyway." Platitudes and small talk. Grady had hinted that he'd kept his sister at arm's length in the offices in New York. "I have to get the barbecue out of the toolshed if you want to walk with me."

"No, I'll go see Grady. I just wanted to thank you." She looked less confident. "Do you think he'll let me in?" She twisted her fingers together in a nervous gesture.

"Of course, he invited you, right?"

"Yes, but he's been so difficult to read. To be honest, I'm not exactly sure what I did to get his silent treatment. I don't want to make things worse." She sighed, looking distressed. She clearly loved her brother and this estrangement had cost her.

"Grady needs to explain himself," Farren said gently because she didn't have a clue what had come between Grady and his sister. She'd never asked, and he'd never offered an explanation other than Delphine was meddlesome. "When you clear the air with him, you'll both feel better, I'm sure of it." She clasped the other woman's upper arms and gave her a light squeeze of encouragement. "You'll be fine. You'll come through this."

Delphine squared her shoulders. "I hope so. I miss my brother." With that, she turned on her heel and headed toward Grady's private entrance.

GRADY DISCONNECTED from his virtual meeting as a knock came at his door. Must be Farren stopping in to say hello. He ran his palm over his hair to smooth it and went to answer. But the woman framed through the door's window wasn't Farren.

Delphine. *Of course she'd race over right away.* He toyed with sending her away, but it was time to come clean. He wasn't happy about it, though.

He opened the door, scanning the pool area as he did so. Farren wasn't anywhere in view, but the pool was full of screaming, laughing children. *Huh.*

"Here I am, in the flesh, and we're alone. We can talk. Or not." He walked toward the living room, leaving Delphine to step in. "Shut the door, I don't want to hear all the screaming from the pool."

She followed him inside. "Nice to see you, Grady," she sing-songed. "Nice to see you, too, sister dear."

He turned to face her, chuckling. "Okay, I've been a total jerk and I'm, uh, sorry." And he realized he was telling the truth, the honest-to-God truth. Rather than be open with her about Veronica, he'd retreated further while he came to terms with all he knew.

But what he'd learned wasn't Delphine's fault. They'd both been taken in. He opened his arms and she stepped into them.

"Twins shouldn't be apart that way," she said with a sniff. "It's not natural." Her shoulders slumped against him. "Whatever I did, Grady, I'm sorry."

The twin thing was more Delphine's joy than his. She was his sister and he loved her. But she'd loved being a twin and swore that gave her more incentive to make sure he was happy.

"But you couldn't resist doing it again with Farren, could you?"

"What do you mean?" She pulled back and looked up at him.

"You sent her to me to set us up, the way you hired Veronica and put her in my overworked sights."

She rolled her lower lip out in a classic childhood expression. "And you wanted to marry Veronica in the end. So, even though she's gone, she was the right choice for you. I don't understand how you can blame me for her accident."

He shook his head. This would be a long and difficult conversation. "I didn't blame you for that at the time and I don't blame you now. But there are things about Veronica you don't know." He settled himself to explain. It was time.

She reared back. "What do you mean?"

He headed for his lounger and sat with his hands over his belly. He waved her to the futon where she settled and curled her legs up beside her.

"About three months ago, I heard from a man I didn't know." The guy had waited until his guilt had peaked about six weeks after Veronica's drowning. "But Veronica did."

She tilted her head, curious. "And?" Her brows held a small knit that heralded confusion.

Grady drew a deep breath. "He was Veronica's lover, the man she was paddling across the lake to see that night."

"You can't be serious." Her eyes went wide with disbelief and shock. She laid a palm over her belly as if she felt queasy. "I don't understand." She shook her head in denial, but he knew his sister and she was already putting pieces together in her mind.

"Want a coffee? Or water."

"No." She paled. "I need to hear the rest." She leaned down and moved her purse. Moved it again. Agitation meant she couldn't settle, so her purse took the brunt as she lifted, dropped, and slid the heavy weight of it from side to side. He knew it weighed heavily; she carried half her belongings in that bag. "Tell me plainly what happened."

He nodded and caught her gaze. Held it. "Out of the blue, I got a call from a man in tears. The number looked vaguely familiar, as if I should know who it was on the other end, so I answered. The guy was blubbering, nearly incoherent. It was so unexpected that I didn't hang up right away."

"But you didn't know the number?"

He shook his head. "Maybe I'd seen it in Veronica's contact list or something. The crying made me wonder if it was a wrong number, but what if this guy was suicidal? I kept him talking, asking about his life, and pointing out that people loved him." He shrugged, feeling the remnants of his helplessness at the time.

She nodded. "That must've been awkward and strange." She clucked her tongue in that way she had of expressing concern.

"What do I know about this stuff?" He went on. "I've seen people talked off ledges and bridges on television and movies. That's it." The fear he'd felt with his initial contact rattled through him again, like muscle memory or something.

"Of course." She nodded, hanging on each word. "Anyone would do the same."

"But then he said that the only one who loved him had drowned. I went on alert. Like, what are the odds, right?"

"Not high." She shook her head and looked unbearably sad.

"When I asked how he got my number, he said he got it from Veronica's phone when she was sleeping." He'd said it so calmly, as if Grady should already know that he'd seen her sleeping. But Grady's mind had raced and rebelled at the idea of some other man seeing his fiancée asleep. Things had unraveled quickly from there.

"I thought the guy was pranking me —like a weirdo who gets his kicks getting into the heads of the bereaved, or—" He drew in an uneasy breath and dragged both hands through his hair. He had to finish this.

She nodded. "I'd wonder the very same thing. Anyone would." Clasping her arms around her waist, his sister rocked in distress. "But he wasn't doing that, was he?"

Grady shook head. "When Veronica took the job with me, she told her boyfriend, *this guy*, about the long hours and the travel. After a few weeks, he came up with the idea that she should be available to me." Saying it out loud like this made him squeamish. He couldn't overlay the woman he'd loved with the woman this man claimed she was.

"Veronica *planned* to seduce you?" Delphine asked, her voice faint with shock. "It's hard to believe she could do that while involved with someone else. Not the woman I knew." Her words dripped of betrayal and rising anger.

"Not at the beginning, but after a few weeks. It wasn't her idea, but yes, she enticed. Invited. And yes, seduced me. I hesitated because I had to be certain of her signals. I walked a minefield with her and all along, she must've been laughing at me trying to keep things professional. But she was subtle, and I didn't see how she manipulated each situation. I don't want to blame her, a woman who worked for me. Ordinarily, I'd never look at an employee that way, but she was perfect for me. Veronica was all I wanted in a wife."

"Do you think she targeted you before she applied for the position?"

"No. This was an opportunity for her. For them." He shook his head. There'd been some honest affection for him. He felt sure of it. "I saw exactly what she wanted me to see. A fabulous assistant, with my best interests at heart. A woman I could partner with in business and in life. She suggested a pre-nuptial agreement once. She looked as if she hated the idea and by then, I was caught up in how lucky I was to have found the perfect woman right under my nose."

"And all that time, this man was waiting for her. I'm so sorry. I feel sick." She covered her mouth for a long moment. Got control and waved him to continue.

"For our divorce, yes. They saw each other whenever she said she needed to visit her family. Which was once a month; sometimes twice. The other day at her parents' house I learned she went months between visits. She must've been with him, instead." He shrugged, feeling sympathetic. "I know this is a shock. It was for me, too. I grieved for weeks in this house and steered clear of people. I knew wherever I went, people at the office, our clients, everyone would look at me with pity. I couldn't face it." The memories of the weeks after their mom's death had crowded his mind. School, sports, girls, his buddies. Everywhere he looked he'd seen awkward sympathy.

"I get that. I do. Veronica was with you at home, work, away on business with you. She was like your other half." Her eyes filled and she dabbed at them. When she raised them again, they were filled with outrage on his behalf. He shook his head at her.

"A few weeks in, I'd wallowed enough and felt ready to return to work, except I got his call. Jeremy. He wouldn't give me his last name, but he was wracked with guilt and had to confess. I listened to the whole thing, numb.

"He said it was his idea to rent a cabin across the lake so she could paddle over. She didn't want to chance that she'd be missed, but when her bridesmaids went to their rooms, she took the canoe, too tipsy to handle it.

"Jeremy told me he'd insisted on seeing her that night. Told her they deserved to drink champagne and celebrate their win over me. He has a lot of guilt to live with." Grady shook his head. "Of course, he blames himself for her death."

"But why call you? Why put this in your mind? He unloaded on you."

"I don't know. But in a strange way I think he may have wanted to apologize or let me know that she'd never really been mine. I can't get clear on his motive." He shrugged. Jeremy's reasons for telling Grady the truth were his.

"Maybe a bit of both. By telling you everything he can punish you and himself." She frowned. "You haven't heard from him again, have you?"

Grady shook his head. "His number's out of service. And I didn't get his last name."

"I'll take a ginger ale if you have some. It'll settle my stomach," his sister said softly. "This new version of Veronica will take some time to get used to." She gasped. "I'm so sorry I put her in your path."

Grady went to the fridge and dug out a can of ginger ale. He found a glass, filled it with ice. "Not your fault. I needed an assistant, and you handle HR for the firm."

After he delivered her drink, they sat in silence while Delphine digested all he'd told her. After a moment, she spoke. "Grady. I don't know what to say to make this better. How did your month go at work?" He saw residual pain in her eyes, but at least now she understood why he waited to explain himself.

"Pretty much as expected. A lot of searching glances from staff, brusque concern from clients. Murmurs of condolences from everywhere. Sorry I cut you off so often, but I wasn't ready to discuss this. Especially not at the office." Not in New York, where most of his time with Veronica was spent.

No, he had to wait to be here in Last Chance Beach. He wanted to be home when he exposed himself this way.

"And all along you had this secret. This terrible secret." She reached across the distance and patted his knee. "I'm sorry I ever meddled. I thought she was perfect for you, and I had hopes you'd hit it off. I was careful to say what I knew you wanted to hear regarding an assistant." She paused and drew a deep breath. "Have you told Farren?"

"No. I wasn't sure I could get through telling you." His fake girlfriend didn't need to know any of this. But he could see why Delphine would ask. She believed he and Farren were the real thing.

Chapter Fifteen

FARREN SAT WITH DENNY outside his unit as they watched his oldest boy and middle boy line up to get a hot dog and a bag of chips. The baby was asleep inside and the door at their backs sat open in case she woke from her nap. Denny expected to hear her at any moment.

"The boys won't stand near each other," Denny lamented as each boy looked stiff and unyielding, cold shouldering each other.

"They're strangers, right?"

"I guess. But they've known about each other for months. They've both said they forgive me." The boys moved up a place in line.

She chose to be forthright with Denny because they went back so far and if he didn't like it, he could leave. "Let's face it; you needed them to say they forgive you, so they did. They said what you wanted to hear."

He stared at her, then blinked. "Don't pull your punches, Farren. Give it to me straight," he said sourly. His shoulders sagged, but he stayed seated. He'd probably been lectured by every other woman in his life.

He didn't need another lecture. He needed someone to help him move on from here. With his children. Farren had no ax to grind, no personal pain to excise. Fair enough.

"Talking around the issues won't help," she said. "You all need honest conversation. Forgiving you doesn't mean your sons are willing to accept each other yet." She was blunt, but he needed to hear the truth. "They need time, and this weekend is just the beginning. A year from now, they'll be accustomed to each other. Maybe not best buddies, but they'll have come to terms with the changes." She hoped. Her heart broke for Denny's children. Their loss of innocence, their sense of betrayal and anger.

"You were always wise, Farren. That was one of my favorite things about you." He gave her a lopsided smile. "Sometimes I wish I'd never left town."

"I'm glad I stayed."

His eyes filled with affection she didn't want. Not from him. She looked toward the breezeway and wondered what Grady was doing.

"We should've gone to college together," Denny said. "I don't know why we didn't." He shook his head and she realized he didn't remember that he hadn't asked her.

She watched the two boys. The older one, Jamie, was tall and long limbed while the younger looked like a small tank. Billy was sturdy and solid. Neither boy smiled and their body language was stiff and pained. They were handed their hotdogs at the same time and moved to the table set up with condiments.

Billy set his bun on the table and the dog immediately rolled off the bun, then the table, and hit the ground. The shock on his face was comical and Denny snorted. "Poor kid. I better go help. He's gonna blow up over that. He loves hot dogs, and his mom won't let him have them."

She placed her hand on Denny's arm. "No, wait."

Denny subsided into his chair as he watched Billy and Jamie. "Are you kidding me? I can't believe it."

"I think, in the long run, things will work out," she said softly. She blinked away a tear.

Jamie had handed Billy his hot dog and moved back to the barbecue to ask for another for himself. Despite all that the boys needed to adjust to, Jamie the only child had suddenly become a big brother.

Billy's face looked thunderous at the kindness, but his expression turned to acceptance as he watched Jamie get another hotdog for himself.

There may have been the flash of a small smile between the boys.

"They'll have to work things out themselves, won't they?" their father said. "I can't make this easier for them, or tell them to just do it, or make them be friends."

"You can encourage and support them and explain yourself if they ask. And love them just as they are."

"All of that sounds easy, but I messed up bad and nothing about these kids will be simple." He looked at her with eyes that brimmed with tears. "But I'll give it my best shot."

GRADY AND DELPHINE stepped out of his door to watch the gathering of children and adults for the barbecue. Nothing smelled quite like grilled dogs. Nothing made people smile quite like them, either.

"Is that Farren across the way?" Delphine asked, although there was no mistaking her. She looked to be in a serious conversation with Denny whatsisname.

"Yes."

"Who's that man she's sitting with?"

"I think they must be friends from another time. He brought kids with him."

Delphine cocked her eyebrow. "I see."

He gave her a side-eye. "Farren had a life before you threw her into mine."

"She's never been married. Doesn't date much. She told me so." His sister frowned. "But they look cozy," she said as they watched Farren slip her hand to the guy's forearm.

"Yeah, they do." He frowned and felt a tightness in his chest. "She'll tell me about him later."

"I hope she does. After what you told me about Veronica, I'm doubting my judgment."

He snorted. "Tell me about it."

"Wait a minute," she said consideringly. "If he's here with kids, then he's here for Singles Fest, right?"

"I would assume so."

"Then he's looking for a wife and mother for his children." Delphine turned to him, her shoulders square and her back straight. "Who better than a woman he's known before who doesn't have children of her own? Someone kind and sweet like Farren."

His sister had echoed his thoughts. "She'll tell me about him later," he said, repeating himself. And for reinforcement, he said it again in his head.

AFTER A QUICK SHOWER and a change of clothes into a comfortably loose summer dress, Farren knocked on Grady's door. This visit was much later than she'd planned because the time she'd given Denny had eaten into her evening. She was tired, but excited to share all that had happened with Grady.

After the Fourth of July parade, she had a dinner at The Captain's Table planned for the adults. They'd needed a full complement of babysitters, but Eva had pulled it off.

She waited for Grady to answer his door, but no voice sounded from inside. Maybe he'd given up on her and gone out. As far as she knew he hadn't come looking for her since he'd arrived. But he'd likely been hard at work and catching up with Delphine. She wanted to believe he was here for her, but it was more likely that he was putting on a show of support so Delphine would believe their lie.

She knocked again. If he didn't answer, she'd walk through the breezeway and take a look up to the balcony over the veranda in case he was up there.

She hoped Grady and Delphine had cleared the air between them. Siblings shouldn't be at war. Her brothers had certainly caused her grief as they'd grown up, but she couldn't imagine anything coming between them now.

Even if she hadn't seen Grady for long, she'd been aware of his presence all day. While talking with Denny, she'd been warmed by the idea that at the end of her day, she'd have Grady to talk to. She wouldn't betray Denny's confidences but unwinding with Grady would smooth some of her disappointment in her old boyfriend and concern for his innocent children. She'd mention Denny, of course, but she'd never share the details of the mess his life had become.

Wired and too excited to sleep, she needed to unwind and talk some things through before she settled in for the night. Hoping Grady hadn't given up on her and gone out, she raised her hand to knock one more time when the door opened with a flourish.

She gasped because suddenly she was face to face with Grady who held out a gorgeous display of flowers. Lilies, roses, and Chrysanthemums with Baby's Breath to separate the color palette filled the cellophane wrap in his hands.

"Oh, you didn't!" He placed the bouquet into her waiting hands, and she held them to her nose to sniff. "These are too much. You shouldn't have."

He crowded her to step outside, confusing her. She'd assumed they'd talk in the house.

Over the sweet-smelling bouquet, she saw his eyes light up. "I'm proud of how you brought this together so quickly. You're amazing, Farren."

"Oh, thank you, but I couldn't have pulled this off without you. And Eva." She wanted to cry with gratitude. "And even Delphine helped me with the job interviews."

"I feel like a jerk for not seeing your dream immediately." He shook his head and turned to lock his door. He was dressed in cargo shorts and a Hawaiian shirt and smelled better than any man had a right to.

"What's happening? I thought we were going to talk. But if you have plans, that's fine," she embarrassed herself by asking. He had somewhere to be, and she'd held him up waiting for her.

"I have plans, all right," he said with a mysterious smile that looked half mischievous.

"What are you up to?" She demanded as he turned her shoulders to face the pool.

"Walk this way." He urged her gently forward, toward the center court. When she set off, he kept his right hand on her right shoulder. He tugged her close to his side. Held this way, she could smell his aftershave and feel the heat of his body.

Warmth and support emanated from Grady into her weary, overexcited mind. She was too tired to think and his arm around her felt like heaven. Her conversation with Denny had been emotional and she felt the aftereffects. But she still couldn't share. That was okay. Denny would work things out on his own. He had to learn to clean up his own mess.

"I've missed you," she blurted, stupidly. They'd only been together a handful of times, but nothing she'd done for Singles Fest had happened without her wondering what Grady would think of it. Every night he'd applauded her decisions or offered a different, male, view of her business.

"We've talked at night for a month. That's more talking than we did when I was here," he said. "More talking than I've done with any other woman."

That seemed an odd comment, considering he'd been engaged. "Yes, but we know each other better because of our late-night chats."

"That's true," he said, with a slight squeeze on her shoulder.

"Why are we leaving the property?" They'd stepped onto the wooden walkway, heading for the beach. Up ahead she saw fancy lanterns set in the sand. "Oh, my!" She stopped dead. "What have you done?"

On the sand, surrounded by two-foot-high lanterns, sat a table set for two. Ladder back chairs sat kitty-corner to each other so the occupants could watch the distant waves. As she drew nearer, she saw fine linen, and a flowered centerpiece.

"Oh, Grady. This is lovely." She recognized the table, chairs, and linens from The Captain's Table, at the Sands. "How?"

As he held out her chair for her, a server stepped out of the shadows with a bottle of champagne.

"Just a small celebration for two," Grady said as he took his seat. "I took the liberty of ordering a light meal. I wasn't sure if you'd grabbed a hot dog or not."

She grimaced. "I didn't have time. But they smelled great."

"I slipped out toward the end and grabbed one," he confessed. "Nothing like a hot dog on the Fourth of July weekend." He held up his champagne flute. "To success and dreams coming true."

"Thank you." She tapped her glass to his and took a sip. "Crisp and delicious."

A green salad appeared on a plate in front of her, and another landed in front of Grady. The server was quietly efficient; she'd hardly noticed the arrival of the food. "How did you arrange all this?"

She forked up some lettuce and a cherry tomato and found it had been drizzled in her favorite dressing. The kitchen at the Sands knew her preferences because she'd worked at the hotel. James, the chef at The Captain's Table had a knack for remembering details.

"Thank you. This is so thoughtful." She smiled, feeling warm all over at this special touch. "I appreciate this." *This* was the perfect ending to a stress-filled, exciting, and emotional day. Between the pressure of the launch and chatting with Denny, she was exhausted on all levels.

Care and attention to detail were what the Sands was known for, but this seaside meal was superb. From the table setting, lanterns, and the food, it was perfection.

"It seems as if I've been running all day," she explained. "My head is a whirl of thoughts, trying to see if I missed anything today or forgot something for tomorrow. And now, here we are, sharing a quiet meal in a romantic setting." She smiled because it was all so perfect. *He* was perfect. "You've outdone yourself on the fake boyfriend front." The last was said in a joking tone because they both knew this was done for the rumor mill and not because he felt romantic. Not when he'd lost his fiancée only months before. "You know the chef is a major source of gossip in town."

He shook his head. "I did not know that, so I guess this meal works for more than one reason."

She wondered about his other reason for going to all this trouble, then set the wonder aside. He was being gracious on her launch day. End of story.

"From the laughter and the squeals coming from the pool and playground, I'd say you hit all the right notes for your clients," he was saying. "This was their first evening. Some have driven for hours, others flew in, but you gave them what they needed, a way to blow off steam and have fun." He chuckled. "And grilled hotdogs."

She cocked her eyebrow at his change of attitude. "You didn't mind the sound of children and families?"

He shrugged and chuckled. "I think I've grown since I made those comments." His teasing tone coaxed a smile from her. "What else happened today? Any surprises with the guests?"

"A boy asked if we had swimming lessons planned and I asked Eva if she could arrange some. It was a great suggestion, and we'll list them in the future. Even if kids only learn to keep their head above water or float, it'll be a win."

"Great plan," he said with a nod. "That's something kids won't forget. Most people remember when they learned to swim. They'll clamor to come back and if the parents have a good time, you'll have repeat business."

"It will also be good for Last Chance Beach. Families will return even if it's not a Singles Fest weekend."

He winked at her and then for a few moments they focused on their salads and as soon as they finished, their plates were whisked away.

"Another thing happened today," she offered as she recalled her time with Denny. "An old friend from high school arrived with his children."

"Oh?" Grady thanked the server for their entrees. Steak and small roasted garlic and rosemary potatoes and delicate asparagus spears topped with almond slivers filled the plate.

She drank in the scent of the food. Her mouth watered. "I thought you ordered a light meal?"

"The steak is half-size. And the potatoes and asparagus are lunch portions." He picked up his knife and fork. "I'm famished. I ate on the plane hours ago and the hot dog I snagged off the grill is long gone."

"The meal may be lunch sized but the bread is fresh-baked and that's temptation beyond resistance for me." The French loaf from the Sands baker was heaven wrapped in a delicate crust.

"That's what the chef said. He made sure you'd have all your favorites."

Warmth spread through her at Grady's efforts to give her this perfect meal in this perfect setting.

"I wonder if I could offer this to the group." She looked around the beach, felt the gentle salt-scented breeze and sighed with the peace of it. A gentle roar came on the breeze as the waves lapped the shore. "We could set up more lanterns and have four or five tables set apart for privacy. The Sands could cater if people ordered in advance from a set menu." Her previously tired brain woke up to the possibilities for romance. "It would have to be an extra charge, of course. Not everyone will want a meal with a special person."

"It could work well for those couples who find someone they're interested in." He followed her gaze around the space with approval in his eyes. "A last evening meal so to speak. Their kids tucked in with a sitter while they enjoy this." He looked pleased with himself, and he deserved to. "Being here would be something to remember when they go home and back to work." He spoke softly as if it meant the same to him.

When he returned to her, he focused on her eyes. And OH! She wanted to lean in for a kiss. But she remembered the truth of their situation just before she made a fool of herself.

He straightened in his seat. His tone changed, became brisk. "You were saying a friend from high school showed up?"

The change of topic and his tone brought her back to reality. "Denny. Yes. He has three children. Two boys and a girl. We dated a bit in school and it's hard to believe he's a single parent."

Not that Denny didn't deserve to suffer for what he did, because she believed in fidelity and honesty. He'd lacked in those areas, the most basic of relationship rules. Not once, but twice and at the same time. The pain he'd caused was immeasurable. Unforgivable. For the first time, she was glad he'd left her behind when he left for college. She smiled to herself and let a small piece of her heart heal an almost forgotten wound.

"Time moves on and life happens," Grady said with a bland expression and a shrug. Of course, Grady assumed Denny's situation was typical. One divorce from one woman typical. "Nice guy?" The question was blithe and dry.

"I always thought so," she replied, ruminating on the strangeness of life. If asked last year if she thought Denny could be anything but what he seemed to be, she'd have sworn he was one of the good guys. His terrible failure of decency was a lot to process. "He's struggling as his children adjust to their new circumstances."

It wasn't fair to say anything more about Denny's poor choices. Grady didn't know him and while the locals would gossip amongst themselves, it was wrong to share the truth about Denny with Grady.

"This steak is marvelous," she said with determination that Grady didn't miss. The change of subject was clear.

Chapter Sixteen

FARREN HAD SWITCHED the conversation to the food to put Grady off asking more about her old friend. *Fine.* Maybe this Denny was more important to her than she let on.

It was tough not to press her, but he held his tongue. They weren't in a real thing anyway. Just this weird, phony place where they talked business and the minutiae of their days. He shouldn't think anything of their late-night talks, but they were a highlight he looked forward to.

Farren's hair caught the flickering lantern light, making it shine and glow with a low luster that drew his eye. Her expressive face moved through her emotions, and he'd read them clearly as she'd talked about Denny.

Right at the top it was plain she had fond memories of him. She felt sorry that he'd landed up a single father. A divorce would be tough on kids. But there was far more to this story than she was saying. The only conclusion was that she was protecting her old boyfriend. He didn't care what Denny's story was, but Farren's desire to protect the guy was a concern.

And then, there were three children in the mix. A woman as softhearted as Farren—well, it didn't take a genius to see which way this could go.

He settled into his meal and when he offered her more wine, she covered her glass with her hand.

"No thanks, I'm sticking to my one glass limit. More than that and I lose control of my tongue."

Something he'd love to see, especially if her loss of control were in his mouth. He'd long ago decided that soon, he'd kiss Farren, and she'd know it meant something more than putting on a show for his sister.

"No more wine," he said, conceding with a smile. Too bad, he might've been able to get her to open up about Denny. "What's on your agenda for tomorrow?"

This was the same question he'd asked every night for the month he was in New York. And each night, she'd given him a brief rundown of her plans for the next day. Sometimes, she succeeded at getting everything done and other times she fell short.

But he heard it all and encouraged her if she faltered and cheered when she succeeded. She'd done the same for him, though his business wasn't something she was familiar with. But the basics were the same as any other real estate transaction, it was just that the number of zeroes was higher.

The grateful look she gave him for accepting the change of topic was worth keeping his questions about Denny unasked. It would be easy to learn more about the guy, but he'd bide his time and see how things panned out. What he really wanted was for Farren to be honest about Denny.

He wouldn't chase a woman who had her sights elsewhere. For now, he'd shelve his plan to kiss her the way he wanted to.

"WE HAD THE MOST ROMANTIC meal ever," Farren told Eva the next morning as Eva prepared for her morning at the pool. They were in Farren's room, and she was looking over her to-do list.

Pool time was this morning while the afternoon was the parade for the Fourth. "Grady arranged a table for two on the beach. He'd ordered a perfect meal from The Captain's Table."

The lantern light had made Grady glow like some sexy movie star. His eyes shone with interest for whatever Farren had to say.

"I'm sure the evening continued back at his place," Eva hinted broadly for details. "After all, he's been away for a month." Her friend waggled her brows suggestively.

"It was a night to remember," Farren replied, trying to put a low thrill in her voice. Eva bent to pick up her towel and water bottle, so she missed the flush on Farren's lying face. She scrubbed at her cheeks so Eva would think she'd rubbed her skin and brought up the pink that way.

"See you later," Eva said as she stepped outside with a brief wave. "I've got extra sitters ready to come at a moment's notice if any more of the clients want adult time. Emails started arriving last night after people met around the pool."

"Success is sweet," Farren said, hoping some of the connections between the adults would stick. But if not, the parents were having fun and getting what they came for.

For her, last night had been a night to remember, just not in the way Farren had made Eva think.

After the wonderful, romantic dinner on the beach, Grady had kept his distance on the way back. She'd leaned toward him with her hand open in an obvious invitation to hold hands, but he'd stopped walking to stare down the beach at something she couldn't see. The moment had been lost.

And then, when they'd come to her door, she'd stood close to him with her face turned up to his. The invitation to kiss her couldn't have been clearer. Thankfully, she'd avoided closing her eyes and pursing her lips to kiss him. That would've been an embarrassment she'd never get over.

Grady had stepped back from her and said, "That was great. Thanks for the update on your day. See you tomorrow."

The evening had fallen flat, and she wasn't sure why. She'd tossed and turned through the night, trying to understand where things had shifted from romantic to business, but was no closer to figuring out the aggravating man AKA Grady the Grump.

Tonight, the adults would have dinner at the Sands. Each course would mean a seat change as the singles mingled, ending with an after-dinner drink and a stroll back along Main to the Landseer. She hoped people would pair off for the walk home through town, but she had a feeling some clients were more cautious than others. At this stage in their lives, their hearts were guarded. Much like hers.

It wasn't that she'd had a big love destroyed, but when she and Denny had been young and she'd thought, *in love*, it had hurt when he'd left without a care for her. Through senior year she'd waited for him to talk about them being together in college, and when that didn't happen, she'd decided not to speak up herself. Instead, after they'd gone to separate colleges, she'd waited for him to talk about life afterward. About him coming back with her to Last Chance Beach. That conversation had never happened, either. They'd talked mostly about how much fun he was having partying. Then even those conversations had stopped as Denny had moved on.

By not asking for more from him, she'd saved herself from the most embarrassing conversation she could imagine. She'd nursed her broken heart on her own. Maybe that had been a mistake, but clearly, Denny hadn't wanted a quiet, accepting girlfriend.

He'd wanted fun and eventually the danger of having two families a state apart.

Denny's transgressions had come home to roost. All indications were that he was interested in rekindling what they'd had in high school. She wasn't sure how to feel. Different emotions surfaced like a water wheel scooping up compassion, loss, regret, anger, even smugness. Sometimes the uppermost emotion was satisfaction that he'd been caught. She didn't like that one, it seemed unkind. But he was wrong to think he could crook his finger and she'd come running. What did he take her for? Some kind of desperate loser? *Pfft.*

She set aside her thoughts of Denny and her emotions around him. There was no time to wallow in the past when her future was at stake. After the morning pool time, she'd escort the group to the town center for the parade. Maybe by then she'd have heard from Grady about joining her for dinner tonight.

Last night he'd been cool and noncommittal after their meal on the beach, but maybe he'd been distracted by business of his own. She couldn't think of a single thing she'd said to him that would cause a wall to grow between them. Maybe she'd imagined his coolness.

She walked to his private entrance and rapped on the door.

GRADY STEPPED OUT OF the shower to the sound of a knock. Wrapping a towel around his hips, he strode, still dripping, into the kitchen to peer through the window.

He double-checked that his towel knot was snug and opened the door to face Farren, looking intent and determined. "Hi?"

"Are you coming to the dinner tonight?" Her purple gaze ran over his chest and bare legs. Her cheeks flushed, pupils dilated, and he realized she liked what she saw.

Good. So did he. She was dressed in a short denim skirt and tight tee with the words Singles Fest stitched into the fabric over her left breast. She looked good enough to eat. *Down boy.*

"I assumed you'd want to go with your friend. Denny, is it?" *Lame, O'Hara. Really lame.* He hadn't wanted to expose his feelings on the man's suspiciously timed reappearance.

She blinked and he saw gears grind behind her eyes. She knew. *Damn.*

"Denny's here to give his children—er—fun together. He's a busy guy and didn't spend much time with them—er—before."

"He's making up for lost time with his children?"

"Sure!"

"So, you're here to ask me to escort you to this group dinner?" She was so beautiful when she blushed. But the blush was a clear signal that, again, she was hiding something about Denny.

"Yes, last night we didn't talk about you escorting me. Will you come with me or not?" She leaned close, bringing her unique scent into the kitchen. He was tempted to reach for her hand and tug her into the house. But she was too busy to spend an hour or two alone with him. He read hesitation in her gaze and in the way her brows pinched.

He eased away from her. "Sorry for the towel. I don't usually answer the door this way, but I know how busy your day is and I figured this must be important if you took the time to stop by."

Her eyes widened. "That's fine, I just thought that with your sister here, we should, you know, be seen in public again."

"Right. For Delphine's sake. Good. I'll meet you there." That was his tried-and-true way of saving time with his busy schedule. He'd meet his dates instead of picking them up, giving him more time on the phone or to check details with a client. With a schedule like his, every minute counted.

He was beginning to hate it. Looking at Farren's glowing face and the happy anticipation in her eyes, he wanted to take back the words and offer to pick her up in a tuxedo with a corsage for her dress. Stupid teenage dreams of romance.

Farren stepped backwards two steps to give him room to close the door. As he shut it, he heard the grating voice of her friend, Denny. "Farren, hi!"

Too late and underdressed to go outside with her, he could only peer out from behind the white gauzy window curtain on the door.

Farren greeted Denny and then crouched to a pretty little girl in the stroller the guy was pushing. The child gave her a big wet grin and patted her cheek. After a moment of mutual connection, Farren rose and walked away beside father and daughter, looking content and happy.

Grady blew out a breath and reached for the phone.

Chapter Seventeen

AT SIX THIRTY P.M. Farren slid the spaghetti strap of her dress to her shoulder and smoothed her hands down her waist. She fluffed the wide skirt and gave it a shake. The black shiny cocktail dress wasn't new, but it was flattering and no one in the group had seen it before. She draped a multi-colored pashmina over her arm and picked up her clutch. The look was not exactly elegant, but nice. Not sexy, but dressy enough.

Plus, it wasn't so fancy that she'd outshine the single moms.

If there was anything she'd observed during her time working at the Sands, it was the lack of up-to-date fashion among single parents. It was one of the reasons she'd wanted to start Singles Fest. She'd been in a unique position to see singles past thirty or forty wanting to find a match but competing with the twenty-somethings dressed to kill was impossible.

Singles Fest would level the playing field and give dads and moms time to truly connect. Pride and excitement rolled through her and brought a smile to her lips. One last check in the mirror and she headed for the door.

A lot rode on the success of tonight's dinner and the million dragonflies in her stomach were proof. They zipped and zoomed and banged into each other in her tummy, but she dared not think too hard about them.

She had twenty-five minutes to return to the Sands. After the parade, she'd spent a couple of hours there preparing for tonight. She had plenty of time to see to last minute details on site.

When she opened her door, she opened her mouth, too. In shock.

Grady stood waiting for her, dressed in a perfect black tuxedo, and holding a corsage box. He stole her breath and she wondered if he'd give it back anytime soon.

Then, he presented the cardboard box on his palm with a flourish and flipped open the lid for her to see inside.

A perfect red rose corsage made up of three half-open blooms and a sprig of delicate Babies Breath filled the container. She gasped at the sight and recognized the elegance that the Beach Rose flower shop was known for.

"I thought about the color you'd choose to wear, and I thought you were the kind of woman to have an elegant cocktail dress. I'm glad to see I was right. You look spectacular. What better to set off your dress than a dark red rose." His gaze roved from the top of her head down to her feet.

"Grady," she breathed, barely able to speak. Spectacular? Hardly. Good thing he took charge and picked the corsage out of the box. He stepped up close, slipped his large hand to just above her breast and started to work the pins through the material. Each brush of his knuckles burnt a trail down to her toes.

Any more of this and she'd be alight with fire.

"It's beautiful. Thank you." She spoke next to his ear because his head was bent as he focused on pinning the rose into place. If she turned her head just so, she could kiss his cheek. Her lips tingled with the urge. "The last time I had a corsage was my high school prom."

He turned his head an inch to look at her, his eyes intent, focused and up close like this, tempting. "Let me guess," he said. "Your prom date was Denny whatsisname."

"And my date tonight is you," she responded softly and brushed her lips ever so lightly against his.

"If I kiss you back, we'll never get to the restaurant," he murmured. He stared at her mouth and something wild inside her broke free.

"Impossible timing," she said. But oh, it was tempting to pull him into her unit and spend hours getting to know his body.

"Seems like," he agreed and straightened, breaking into her sexually charged thoughts. He held out his arm and she linked them together with a smile that barely trembled.

"Do you want to walk, or shall I drive?"

"Let's drive there and walk back. I can kick off my sandals on the way home. I'd like to see if any clients partner up on the stroll back. There's a lot of potential for mutual interest tonight." Couldn't she keep her mind off business for one second? Apparently not.

He chuckled. "I'll say there is. You must have a full house for this dinner. I saw a veritable army of teenagers arriving. Babysitters?"

"Eva worked a miracle and found enough kids who wanted the work. I think we've created a job market. After tonight, those sitters may find themselves working all summer for Singles Fest."

"Let's hope we see some fireworks then, and not the sparkly kind."

His double entendre made her laugh as he held his car door open for her. "The fireworks should be happening when we walk home. I tried to time things out for romance to the max." After the dinner on the beach last night, she understood Grumpy Grady understood romance.

She kept her seatbelt from crushing her corsage and bent her head to inhale the delicate rose scent. As her date rounded the hood of the car, her breath caught, and she blinked moisture from her eyes.

This was not real. Grady had his own purpose in pretending they were a thing. She had to remember that. Sure, for now, he was being kind and attentive. He'd spent time getting to know her on the phone, but that was him unwinding after a long day.

If they'd missed a night, he wouldn't have noticed. She ignored all the times he'd called from airports or taxis from distant time zones, telling herself they didn't count.

"When are you going back to New York?" she asked as he backed his rental sedan away from his front door.

He shrugged. "I hadn't thought about it," he said, which was a clearly a lie. A man with his responsibilities would know his own schedule. He'd know where he had to be next week, whether it was New York, or London, or Berlin.

She didn't press him. She had her own responsibilities tonight and she took out her phone to run down her list of reminders. "I have to check that all the tables have place cards, and each table has a sheet of instructions on how the meal will run." This was overkill because she'd put the cards by the place settings herself.

"I'll walk the room with you and check," he said with a brisk nod. "I hope I didn't hold you up too much?"

"No, of course not." She looked down at her chest again. "I love the roses. Did you notice I'm wearing dark ruby shoes?"

"I notice everything about you," he said under his breath.

"Oh, I notice you, too. I've noticed you're not a grump anymore," she offered in a teasing tone. "Not often, anyway."

He gave a small snort of laughter. "I'm trying."

AT THE CAPTAIN'S TABLE, the Sands fine dining restaurant, Grady sat with Farren and Eva at a table for four. Delphine was at the far end of the room, watching things from there. She looked happy chatting with the other people at her table. He leaned into Farren's ear.

"My sister's having a good time. I'm glad she came."

Farren's eyebrow arched. "You didn't expect her to?"

"Hard to believe, but she can be shy around men. I don't often see her openly flirting." Right now she was smiling and engaged in a lively discussion from the looks of things.

"Then my purpose is fulfilled," Farren quipped. "I'll tease her about it tomorrow."

Grady shook his head. "I'd prefer that you not mention it. Despite her bluster and nosiness she keeps her heart guarded."

"So, it's okay for her to make matches for you, but she's careful about romance herself?"

"Exactly."

"Fair enough. I'll see if she brings up a man's name and encourage her if she does."

"Perfect. But then, you always are."

She blushed deeply.

The plan for the meal was standard for singles meet and greet, except most of these people had seen the others at the Landseer. The men moved from table to table between courses, chatting with the seated women. He'd heard a lot of happy conversations and quiet laughter as the group had moved through the ritual.

Which was great except the man who'd been at the table during the entrée had been a huge bore. Now, they were waiting for dessert and coffee, entrée man having risen and moved on already. For the moment it was just the three of them.

Entrée man had not left an impression on Eva. And vice versa. The main part of the meal had brought stilted small talk and bored responses.

It was Grady's fervent hope that no one else had been involved in similar exchanges. Any more of that and the night would fall flat. And he wanted Farren's success. He coaxed a smile from her with a whisper in her ear. "He'll be better with someone else."

Eva leaned in. "I'm dying to know if people have made connections," she said softly. She tilted her head to entrée man as he took his seat at another table.

"I'd say there have been some," Grady replied. "A couple of these men have wanted to know more about you, Eva." But she'd said little to any of them. He wasn't sure why she'd come and agreed to the seat switching game if she weren't interested.

"I saw the same thing," Farren chimed in. "You've been blowing them off."

Eva flushed. "Maybe."

Since Grady hadn't moved to another table it was clear he was here with Farren. She was stunning tonight. Elegant, poised, but warm and caring, too. She was a hit with her clients, who had waved and smiled at them throughout the meal. For once, she wasn't checking lists or her messages. She looked relaxed and happy.

But to the single dads, Eva was fair game. Unfortunately, she'd made it plain she wanted nothing to do with a man with children. It was like a phobia or something. For a woman who provided daycare, and taught swimming and lifeguarded, all aimed at children, he found her curious.

Maybe she didn't want to take on someone else's kids. He shrugged. Fair enough. Not everyone was cut out to be a stepparent.

A server approached and leaned in to talk to Farren. She nodded and looked toward the kitchen. Catching sight of the chef, she smiled. She patted Grady's hand, brushed her lips across his jaw and said, "Duty calls. I want to talk to him about a menu if anyone wants to do a dinner on the beach tomorrow night." She left the table and Grady and Eva were alone.

Grady complimented Eva on her dress, a stark white one that wrapped around her sleek body in some clingy material. "Your next man should be here any second," he said. "But so far no one has passed muster. Am I right?"

"I'm picky, I guess." Eva shifted and tapped her wineglass with the tip of her index finger. "Bored, too, I think."

"Grady," Jesse Carmichael greeted him as he took the seat kitty corner to Eva. "And Eva. It's nice to see you both again." His eyes lit up at the sight of her and Eva shifted under his scrutiny. "You look lovely," he said, drinking in her face. The guy had it bad while Eva looked anywhere but at Jesse.

"Thanks, I haven't seen you at the motel. I didn't think you'd made it, after all." She spoke distractedly and took a sip of wine. Her eyes scanned the rest of the room.

"I'm staying here at the Sands. My in-laws have the children again, so I didn't need the playground." He hesitated. "But maybe I should've brought them. The other parents are saying the place is great and their kids are making friends." He nodded at Grady.

"From the squeals and laughter I hear all day, I'd say that's right." Grady chimed in.

"Farren should be back shortly," Eva said, tapping her wineglass again. "Dessert is on the way."

Jesse looked at Grady, resigned acceptance in his eyes. Eva couldn't have been less interested.

"I think I'll skip dessert." Jesse made to rise, but Eva made a sound that stopped him.

"You should stay," she said. "I guess you're enjoying your time alone. Without the hubbub of three children, I mean. Two boys and a girl? Or do I have that backward?"

"Backward. My girls are seven and eight and my wife believed our next would be a boy. She was so determined to have a son." He shrugged. "Turns out, she was right. Tyler is four. And I'm glad the girls are older. Sometimes, they're the only ones he'll listen to, unless they're the ones he's torturing." He chuckled. "But the girls handle anything he dishes out."

Her eyes seemed to glaze over, and Jesse swallowed his next words. Silence reigned as Grady searched for small talk and came up empty. He'd step away, but Eva looked desperate, and he didn't feel right leaving her if she was having a hard time.

"It's nice that your in-laws keep them sometimes," Eva commented vaguely when it was clear the conversation had stalled.

"Recently, they've been having them sleep over regularly. They're retiring soon and want to spend more time with them. I'll have more time to myself." He locked his gaze with Eva's and Grady glanced away.

The look between his tablemates had taken an intimate turn that surprised him. Eva hadn't struck him as a woman only interested in a good time, but he'd been wrong about women before. Maybe she wanted no strings. He mentally shrugged and tuned out the conversation.

He checked on Farren's whereabouts. She'd moved on from talking with James, the chef, to chatting at Denny's table as she made her rounds. Denny was giving her a huge smile and making her laugh, which felt like a cheese grater against Grady's spine.

He wanted to march over and lay claim to his date, but good manners stopped him and a scene like that might ruin the biggest event on Farren's roster.

The woman sitting with Denny touched his hand, reminding him of her presence. To his credit, Denny shifted gears immediately and brought all his charm to his dessert date. He leaned in toward the woman and brought a deep smile and soft blush to her cheeks.

Dessert arrived, a huge slice of apple pie and ice cream, perfect for the Fourth of July weekend. With a happy hello to Jesse, Farren settled in beside Grady. She vibrated with excitement.

"Tell me." He demanded in her ear. "What's happening? People look happy." *She* looked ecstatic.

"Compliments from everyone," she said quietly. "People are making plans for adult time tomorrow. See all those people on their phones? They're hitting the scheduler and booking the beach dinner. James and I talked about it and he's excited. They'll offer three courses with three entrees to choose from. The babysitters are booking up fast."

"Tomorrow morning it's minigolf, right?"

"Right. Barnacle Bill's. Tee off starts at ten. I think the place will be swarmed." She looked so pleased Grady couldn't help but smile back.

"I'm so grateful to you for helping me out there. I could've taken the group to Summerville, but I want our events to be contained to the island."

"No problem. It was a phone call to an old friend." He grinned at a memory. "We went there as teens. I think I got my first kiss behind the windmill," he said with a smirk. "I was thirteen and she was a year older and half a foot taller than I was."

"That's sweet," she said and gave him an affectionate shoulder bump. "If you get a hole in one, maybe it'll happen for you again." The teasing light in her eyes gave him hope.

"I'll head over there and start practicing right after I walk you home." He loved the old-fashioned concept of walking his girl home. Seeing that she was safe.

Farren pouted prettily and for a moment he stilled at the sight. She seemed to be everything he wanted in a woman.

But then, so had Veronica.

A man's laughter rang out and he checked it out over his shoulder. Denny was making quite an impression on the woman he was with. When Grady turned back to Farren, she watched Denny with a keen eye. Her intent expression made him think Farren didn't like what she was seeing.

He'd never seen himself as a jealous man. But then again, his short-term women hadn't meant much, and Veronica had never been flirty with anyone but him. She'd been circumspect and respectful of their business relationship and never would've brought that side of her into a business dinner or event.

No, he'd been convinced that he was the only man who saw her feminine side.

He snorted and Farren startled at the sound.

"Are you okay?"

"Peachy, just peachy."

Chapter Eighteen

AT THE END OF THE DINNER at nine-thirty, Farren and Eva shepherded the diners out of the restaurant. Eva drifted away into the crowd and Delphine was nowhere to be seen. Farren had Grady all to herself.

As they exited the hotel, and spilled into the cooling night air, Grady grasped Farren's hand and raised it to his lips for a kiss. "From the smiles I'd say the night was a wild success."

"Thank you," she gushed, thrilled with the dinner and the way his lips felt on her knuckles. He was pulling out all the stops. Anyone looking on would believe he was interested in her. For real interested, not just putting on a show. "Dinner went better than I hoped. And some people stayed back to have a drink at the bar."

Being this close to the ocean meant the darkness had cooled the air and the breeze that curled around the building made her shiver.

"Here, let me," he said, offering to drape her shoulders with her shawl. He stood behind her and settled the soft knit pashmina across her shoulders. "Did you know you have dimples back here?"

She felt his thumbs press behind her shoulder blades. "Yes," she said through a light chuckle. "I know not everyone does, but they run in the family. Until I was twelve, I assumed everyone had them." The way he cupped her shoulders felt comforting and she wanted it to go on and on. But someone burst out into laughter and drew everyone's attention as the group strolled along.

"Thank you." She folded the shawl carefully around her corsage to keep from crushing it. "I'm thrilled to see people pairing off for the walk home." More than one couple held hands, smiling into their partners' faces. Farren's heart soared when she realized what she'd brought into their lives.

Grady jerked his head toward where Denny walked with the last woman he'd been sitting with. They weren't holding hands, but their heads were bent together as if sharing secrets.

"It looks as if your friend has found someone interesting," Grady commented drily.

"Yes, that's Mackenzie Fairfield. She has a daughter who's thirteen." And she'd been single for a year. A teacher, Mackenzie felt guilty for her divorce and the effect it was having on her daughter. They'd taken a few minutes together to chat while they'd been on the walkway to the beach this morning. "I'm not sure looking for a new relationship is a good idea right now," Farren mused aloud. She was echoing what Mackenzie had said to her earlier, so Farren was surprised at the clear signals the other woman was giving Denny.

"Denny's ready and if she is, too, then so be it," Grady said firmly. "And a connection doesn't always last. Some of them end after one night."

She cut him a glance. "I guess." But she made a mental note to chat with Mackenzie. Farren had no right to tell the woman what she knew of Denny's history, but she could encourage her to ask a few questions. "But a one-night stand is difficult with children in your motel room," she remarked.

Grady chuckled. "And since the sitters are only hired until eleven, it would have to be a quickie."

Farren bumped her shoulder to his and laughed. She drew to a stop to look up into his laughing eyes. "Maybe we should offer rooms by the hour next time."

"I do believe the wine has gone to your head, Ms. Parks."

"You think?"

Grady threw back his head and laughed hard enough to draw glances, but the conversation had taken such a silly turn, she joined him. She needed the release, she realized, as the laughter dispersed and left her spent. She wiped her damp lashes as Grady flung his arm across her shoulders and drew her into a one-armed side hug.

Pure affection radiated from his eyes into hers and they shared a long moment of humor.

They strolled the block leisurely, glancing into store windows full of T-shirts, swimsuits, and beach towels. They passed souvenir shops and Main Street Hardware, where Jake Hooper had every size of flag a person could want. She suspected he'd sold out his handheld ones today. Everyone at the parade had been waving them.

She felt mellow and generous. Maybe Grady was right, and the wine had loosened her up. Or maybe it was the man she was with. Grady had become a friend and confidant in the last weeks.

"Thank you for all your help." She glanced at the man who still held her close as they strolled together. "Your advice and kindnesses have helped me achieve my dreams. This summer will lay the groundwork for a great year for Singles Fest and without your help and guidance, I don't know if that would've happened." His heat kept her warm, while his sex-deep voice made her tremble inside.

"Aw, shucks," he teased. "I couldn't resist you, Farren. You had me the first time you came rapping on my windows and peering into my house. The determination in your face was fierce and I knew you wouldn't fail. It's been fun watching you succeed." He sobered. "Not to mention, I needed the kick in the butt you gave me to get out of my house and back into my life."

Of all the things she and Grady had discussed, the painful stuff had been mostly off limits. The world knew of his grief, of course, but she and he hadn't spent time on that. She knew he'd hidden away in Last Chance Beach and that he'd found a new interest in Singles Fest. That much was plain when he'd fixed up the walkway and painted the playground equipment.

For reasons of his own, Grady had embraced her business idea and— conveniently for him —Farren and her new business had prevented more matchmaking from his sister.

When he returned to New York and O'Hara Enterprises for good, they'd tell Delphine their relationship had run its course. No harm, no foul.

She'd miss him, though. More than she wanted to.

But that was the way of things for her. Men liked her. A lot. But never enough. And after a while they moved on. Moved away to bigger things.

A loud pop heralded the first of the fireworks over the ocean and the group stopped to stare in awe as a sparkly explosion overhead rained down yellow and blue and purple starlets of color.

"Ooh! Aah." The universal sound of delight rose from the people around them, as she felt for Grady's hand. She clasped it and gazed skyward, the lights obliterating the stars in the black night sky.

FARREN'S WARM HAND in his, her eyes alight with the colors of the rainbow overhead, made Grady want to drag her into his arms and hold her the way a man holds a woman he cares for.

And he did care for Farren. Maybe more than he should. Maybe more than she'd accept. Especially with Denny back in Last Chance Beach and clearly looking for a new woman. His children needed a mother and there'd be no one better than Farren.

She was sweet, kind, genuinely liked children and loved the idea of family. Most women her age were well on the way to having all that for themselves. He wondered, as he looked at her shining, happy face, if Denny had broken her when he'd left her behind.

But would she give her first love a second chance if he asked? Or would she want to start something new and fresh with Grady?

Something real. They'd come to know each other over these last weeks. She was still one of the prettiest women he'd ever met. Her figure was softly rounded and perfect in his eyes. And he loved her little teasing comments and witty banter. She could tease him out of a dark mood and her smile made his heart answer with another.

Farren Parks was the real deal. But, aside from college, she'd never left her hometown to spread her wings. Apparently, had never wanted to. Still, was New York so far away?

Maybe not in miles, but in attitude and action, the Big Apple might as well be on Mars.

He looked along the street. This strip was still inhabited by mom-and-pop stores, even if those moms and pops were younger and more hip. Last Chance Beach was changing, growing and he liked the controlled growth.

It could be fun to watch a quiet corner slowly wake and stretch to its full potential. His great-aunt had loved this place. Her motel had financed different family businesses over decades. Lending seed money to nephews and nieces had become a side-line for the savvy woman. By the time her investments had paid off, another family member would come up with another business idea and everyone turned to the bank of Aunt Ellen.

He and she had had a special rapport and the motel came to him when she passed. He suspected that she'd also intended for him to continue the family loans as needed.

Maybe that's why he'd let Farren talk him into using the Landseer for her clients. He'd been paying Ellen's kindness forward.

There came one last flurry of loud pops overhead, and the red, white, and blue canopy of sparkling stars heralded the end of the show. Short, sweet, and gorgeous, like Farren.

Her hand wasn't enough to hold. He wanted Farren in his arms. He tugged, her arms wrapped around his waist, and he held her close. She smelled so good, felt so right, sighed as if her heart was in it.

When his hands wandered down her back to settle on her softness, she hugged him harder. Her eyes lit with happy success. They could've been the only two people on the street for all the notice he took of anyone else.

He dipped his head and his lips found home on hers. She parted for him and deepened the kiss. The sweet woman in his arms held a secret fire that licked up his sides and landed in his chest and then moved south. Her tongue touched his lips and he opened, fully engaged now. Hopeful as a teenage boy.

"Farren," he groaned against her mouth and heard her say his name, too.

He lifted his head. Her shawl had slipped, and her exposed shoulders gleamed in the light from a storefront sign. The multi-colored material of her shawl brought out the red in her pouty lips. Her shoulders were smooth and rounded and had teased him all evening. He'd wanted to trace the contours with his fingertip and when he'd seen the dimples on the back, he'd wanted to kiss them.

Was there such a thing as a shoulder fetish? He gave a mental shrug. If there wasn't, there should be.

"You know I'm the only one at the motel without children in my room?"

"Is that an invitation Ms. Parks?" His voice had gone gravel-deep with need.

"Do you want it to be?"

"Don't doubt it for a moment."

Chapter Nineteen

SHE COULD HAVE TONIGHT with Grady. Share his bed, feel his heat, be swept away. Farren looked up into his enticing gaze and wanted more than was smart for a woman like her. He'd be leaving soon and who knew if when he came back—if he ever did—that they'd have the same feelings they shared right now. Tonight.

If she didn't grab what she could, she'd have nothing of this time. Nothing to hold onto of Grady O'Hara. Singles Fest would commandeer her life and energy. New York would swallow him up and he'd go back to meetings with princes and billionaires and tech czars.

There was nothing to keep Grady here in Last Chance Beach—small town, sleepy beaches, vacation backwater Last Chance Beach could never hold a man like him. *She* could never hold a man like him.

But she could hold him for one night. She could love him for one night. Give him all of herself this one time. She sighed and accepted what they had for what it was.

This was a short-term fling. A better-than-average one. Grady would leave, and it would end. To him, she would become a pleasant memory of that time at the beach. That time with the girl he'd helped. She hoped he thought of her occasionally when he married another woman like his first love, Veronica.

She smiled bravely into his handsome face, drawn taut with desire. "So, what do you say?" My place or yours?"

His teeth gleamed with his broad smile. A man who was having a dream come true. "I have a bigger bed."

"Lead me to it."

JULY 5 SIX A.M. THE Landseer Motel

Grady closed the private door with a soft *snick* and turned to face the courtyard. The air was already losing its overnight chill as the sun curved over their little part of the world. He breathed in the salt air and grinned, a man satisfied with life on this fine, fine morning. The leftover glow from his time spent with Farren in his arms made him feel.

Feel.

And it was great. He'd been numb for so long and now he wasn't. He'd felt more in these last weeks with Farren than he had in years. Every day had brought smiles, laughter, warmth to his chilled heart. Farren had mended him in ways he hadn't known he was broken. And now, all his pieces were back together.

He hoped she felt the same way. Complete.

With his beach towel slung over his shoulder, he opened the gate to the pool area. He tossed the towel onto the foot of a lounger and remembered not to dive into the too-shallow pool. Motel pools were not meant for more than laps or play.

Five short laps later a movement at the shallow end caught his eye. He took to his feet, shook the water from his head and smoothed his face. There at the edge sat a boy somewhere in the middle years below ten. Old enough to walk out of his room, certainly. Young enough that his mother or father would look for him.

"Hullo," the boy said. "Nice to meetcha. I'm Topher."

"My name's Grady. Nice to meet you, too. You here to swim laps? I'll take the right side if you are."

The boy shook his head. "I can't swim, but I'm gonna learn today." Topher puffed out his skinny chest. The kid was whip lean and had limbs like a colt and teeth that were fighting for space as the permanent ones pushed through.

"I see. You'll be learning from Eva the lifeguard."

"Yeah," Topher said with some excitement. "How did you know?"

"I'm friends with her and with Farren. Do you know her?"

Big nod.

"You want to learn to float?" He had no idea why he offered, but he didn't want to leave the boy out here alone if he couldn't swim. He scanned the windows of all the rooms. A few had their curtains opened and he saw movement inside.

Topher grinned. "It would help if I already knew how when I get my lesson later."

"It would," Grady intoned seriously. "I could teach you if you want."

"Okay." A cloud crossed his features. "My mom will be out here soon, so that'll be fine." He seemed to have realized he was alone with a stranger. Grady backed up into deeper water to give the boy space.

"How about this," Grady said. "I'll keep swimming laps until your mom's here and then I'll teach you. Don't step into the pool in case I crash into you."

"OKAY!"

After that loud shout, Grady figured half the motel would be looking out their windows. Topher's mom would be outside any minute.

FARREN HEARD A MUFFLED shout through the window and rolled over to see an empty expanse of rumpled bed beside her. Grady had left. She rubbed her eyes, stretched, and then looked around for a note. She slipped into her bra and panties and grabbed her pashmina off the dresser, where she'd tossed it. When she didn't spy a note taped to the bathroom mirror, she wandered into the kitchen wrapped in her pashmina, like a towel.

Thank goodness her unit was right next door and at this time of the morning, it was unlikely anyone would be witness to her scurry home. She refused to think of it as the walk of shame. There was nothing shameful in how or where she'd slept. Grady had been gentle, loving, and affectionate. They'd laughed together, brought each other joy and had snuggled through the night. And then, they'd done it again. Heat rose to her face at the memories.

In short, Grady had been spectacular and all she'd want in a loving partner. She bit her lip at the notion. No, she couldn't entertain words like *partner*. But she wasn't cavalier about sleeping with men. The night had meant a lot to her. *Grady* meant a lot to her. Maybe more than a lot.

She looked out the window in the kitchen door and saw the man of the hour doing laps. He'd left coffee for her with a note stuck on the machine. A hand drawn smiley face. He didn't need to say anything more because she felt the same.

The simple drawing had her grinning back. She watched Grady do another lap and noticed curtains were being opened in several of the units. The day was starting. Single parents didn't have the luxury of sleeping in.

It was time to dress and hustle back to her room. She searched her heart for a shred of guilt over spending the night in Grady's arms.

Finding nothing but contentment, Farren threw her dress on over her head, zipping it halfway up. She balled up her black pantyhose and slipped them into her clutch and then covered up with her pashmina. Slipping into her sandals by the door, she grabbed her coffee mug and headed outside. She'd done nothing more than finger comb her hair and she felt pretty sure she had mascara rimming the skin under her eyes.

Twelve feet separated their doors. The breezeway accounted for eight of those feet. When she reached the corner, she had four feet to go.

But could she make it without a witness? Of course not. Now there were two men in the pool.

Sitting poolside were three boys and a baby in a stroller. If she weren't mistaken, two of the boys were Denny's and the third was the one who'd asked for swim lessons. Great, that meant the other man in the pool was Denny.

His head popped up and he rubbed the water out of his eyes in time to catch sight of her as she stood at the corner hesitating. She raised her chin, stared him in the face, and gave him a brief wave before walking to her own door.

Denny had been on the swim team for a year or two in high school. She'd forgotten that about him. She'd forgotten a lot, it seemed. His need for attention. His selfishness and how easily he acted out when he didn't get his own way. Selective memory. She'd wanted her high school sweetheart to always be sweet. But nothing could be further from reality. He'd proven himself faithless, selfish, and callow. She only hoped he was honest when he said from now on his children would come first.

She frowned and looked over her shoulder at him. Could a person change those ugly personality traits or were they embedded to the bone? Had she been giving him the benefit of the doubt for the sake of his children?

The unanswerable question sat in her mind as she caught sight of Grady lifting the boy who wanted to learn to swim into the shallow end. Topher, his name was Topher, and his mom's name was Val. She smiled as she stood for a moment to watch.

Grady set Topher on his feet in the shallows and got him to put his face in the water. She saw bubbles rise as Grady encouraged him to blow air out through his nose.

Denny went back to his laps and his sons shouted encouragement to Topher as their feet dangled in the water.

GRADY HELPED TOPHER get used to water being in his face and then lifted the boy into his arms. He settled him on his outstretched arms so that he could feel the water beneath his body. "Good, you're doing really good," he assured the boy.

Farren had looked rumpled and kissable as she'd crept out his private door. He hadn't missed the exchange of looks and waves with Denny. But she'd raised her chin and owned the moment, and he couldn't be prouder of her.

For all her ambition and verve, she was a small-town girl with values some might say were old-fashioned. He called them charming and right for her. She'd given herself to him freely and honestly and he'd accepted what she'd offered. His heart had melted a little more with each caress.

Last night had been delicate, heated, and sweet. She had laid claim. Calm, sweet, kind Farren Parks had laid him to waste. Delicately, so at first, he didn't see it. Didn't realize she had him in a powerful grip. And he wanted it again. He wanted *her* again. Being with Farren had renewed him. Sure, it had been a long time since Veronica. But Farren had made him a new man. Different from before. Again, the word *complete* rolled through his mind.

Since she'd pounded on his door and peered into his window looking fierce and determined, he'd changed. He told himself he was kinder, more open, and unexpectedly even-tempered, but he was likely lying to himself.

Whatever. As long as Farren believed the same lie, he was good.

"Mom, Mom, look!" Topher yelled when his mother came to stand poolside. His mother was wrapped in a terry robe that had seen better days and looked like she'd just woken. She yawned and smiled at them.

"I see," she said in a morning rough voice with a big smile. "You're floating." She mouthed a thank you to Grady over the sound of Topher's excited chatter.

"And Grady's gonna let go of me any minute now. But it's okay if I sink, 'cause I can hold my breath."

"Great!" She clapped, looking thrilled.

"He's doing super," the other kids on the pool deck called. Denny's kids, he assumed. The girl with red ringlets bouncing on her head clapped her hands and giggled, drawing Topher's mother's attention.

She bent down and cooed at the child while Denny drew up beside her. He swiped his hands over his head to clear the water. The smile he gave Topher's mom looked predatory.

Grady could be biased, but Denny prowled, looking for opportunities. And this sleepy-eyed, comfort-oozing woman was now in the prowler's sights.

Topher kicked his legs and brought Grady back to his purpose. Taking the hint, Grady lowered his arms a couple of inches so that he was barely supporting the boy.

Denny was speaking to Topher's mother, and she responded with shy smiles while a blush bloomed on her cheeks. She distractedly smoothed her bedhead while Denny's daughter giggled.

"Mom! Lookit me," Topher called, interrupting the chat at the edge of the pool.

Denny walked back to join Grady and the boy.

"Did you have a good time last night?" Grady asked the other man. Did he really need to remind the man that he'd been cozying up to a different woman after dinner?

"Yeah," he said. "I paid our sitters to stay longer, and we hit the beach for an hour of private time." His smile turned lecherous as he recalled his apparent success with his dinner companion. "I guess it's cheaper for you since you don't have kids, right? And neither does Farren."

"What do you mean by that?"

"I mean it looks like you beat me to it with her. But no worries, there. I messed up back in the day and shouldn't have thought she'd take me back without a penalty." He shrugged as if losing out on Farren was easy. As if Farren spending the night with Grady was out of spite.

And it hit Grady hard. His arms tensed and Topher felt it.

"Am I okay?" The kid asked, sounding nervous.

"Sure, you are. I'm letting go now and you'll be fine." The boy's body dropped a bit, but he kept his face out of the water. "Good boy," Grady said, as he stepped back slowly, giving Topher room to move his arms and kick his legs.

His mother clapped. "You'll do great with your lesson later," she called.

Other doors in the units were opening as more guests were rousing. Several parents held steaming mugs and settled into their chairs in front of their windows. Some were joining others as children began heading toward the pool or the playground. Not only were people partnering up, but new friendships were being made.

His quiet time in the pool was over, but he was in no hurry to disappear into his house. He looked at Farren's door, wondering if she expected him to check in with her. She may not appreciate the public display.

Grady pulled himself up to sit on the edge of the pool. Denny wheeled his daughter's stroller over to where Grady sat. Denny's boys had run off with friends to the playground.

Topher splashed and practiced on his own. Grady kept watch as the boy showed more confidence.

"About Farren," Denny began. "It's true we have a history, but it wasn't a big thing for me at the time. She was sweet and nice and kind. A great girl. But I wanted a bit of wild and when I headed off for college, I found what I was looking for. And then, after I got married, I found it again."

"You cheated." Grady frowned. Farren had dodged a bullet with Denny. He hoped she knew it.

"More than simple cheating. I'm not proud of what I did. I've messed up a lot of lives. And I'm glad, for her sake, that Farren's wasn't one of them. She's doing great." The other man cleared his throat. "The oldest boy is with my wife. My legal one. The other kids are from my common-law wife. I understand now that basically, I'm a bigamist. I had two families at the same time."

Grady turned his head to stare at the other man, barely keeping his mouth from dropping open.

Denny blew out a long breath and looked to the sky. "That's the first time I've ever said the word aloud. Bigamist. It doesn't sound as destructive as it is. And I never thought of what had happened as bigamy."

"Not what had happened. *What you did.* There's a difference."

Denny nodded. "I've had the difference explained plenty."

Grady sat frozen, staring at Farren's door, hoping she'd stay inside and never have to look at Denny again. He wanted to protect her from hearing any of this. Did she know? Had she heard? And those boys of his. This happy little girl in the stroller. What would they make of their father?

Thoughts raced and turned and crawled over each other, until he realized Denny expected something from him. A response of some kind. Something other than pure disgust.

"I assumed she told you about me," Denny was saying.

"No, she didn't. But you're right, Farren is good and kind." That was probably the reason she hadn't shared. He felt like a fool for being jealous.

"Everyone in Last Chance Beach knows," Denny said. "The locals, I mean. I shouldn't have come here, but it's time for my children to know each other and this seemed like a safe place."

Grady had nothing to say. His thoughts swirled as he stared into the pool. What could he say to a guy who'd messed up so royally?

The quiet of the morning was gone and it was time to check in with Farren. He felt as if they had a lot to talk about. But as he made to rise, Denny spoke again.

"Farren was way too good for me back in school. I knew she wanted us to go to the same college, to plan our lives, but I didn't care. I used her and left her." He shook his head. "It feels like someone else did that, not me. Not the guy who's learned his lesson." He was blinking rapidly, and Grady made sure to look away, toward the office. Denny needed to collect himself.

After a long moment of two strangers staring into the middle distance, a protective streak rose and Grady bit out his next words. "You thought you could come back here and what? Take her off the shelf. Wind her up like a doll."

Except Grady had met her by then, had spent a month of evenings talking with her. Just talking. His heart warmed. Those late-night calls had meant a lot to him. And to her.

"Not exactly. It'll take time, but Farren's worth waiting for. She's sympathetic and if it weren't for you, she'd be more agreeable to seeing me after this weekend." Denny turned and sized him up.

"You said earlier you were glad you didn't mess up her life. But you want to have another chance to screw with her? Break her heart?" His voice went hard. What he'd really like to do was grab this jerk by the collar and—but since Denny wasn't wearing a shirt—and Grady wasn't a violent man—he controlled himself.

"No. But with Farren, I can fix my life. She could help me with my kids, be a good stepmom. Be an *agreeable* wife." Denny shrugged. "If you don't want to take her to New York with you, then let me know. Do a guy a favor."

Do a guy a favor. "Right. Do you a favor and ruin a perfectly wonderful woman." He ground out the words. This— *this!* — was the information Farren had held back about Denny. The bigamy, the mess he'd made for his sons to clean up. They were old enough to understand that their father had betrayed them and their mothers. Red Ringlets was too young to be angry. A blessing for her.

"Hey, you'll be leaving soon," Denny whined. His eyes assessed him and clearly missed Grady's boiling rage. Maybe he was used to the reaction and was numb to it. "A business likes yours needs babysitting. If you take Farren with you, she'll be alone all the time." He shook his head sadly. Then he opened his hands to the obvious. "With me, she'll have a family, a man who comes home at night. She deserves the best and what's better than a guy who's lost it all once and learned from his mistakes?"

He couldn't commit murder, so Grady got to his feet. He leaned down to the toddler in her stroller and waved his index finger in her face to get a grin. She giggled. "Good luck, kid. You're going to need it. And steer clear of any boys who remind you of dear old dad."

He needed to shower off the idea of Denny Bracken making a serious play for Farren and decide how to move forward with her himself.

Chapter Twenty

THE SHOT HE'D TAKEN at Denny as Grady left the pool, rang true. That happy, pretty, little girl had a sorry excuse for a father and would likely judge men by Denny's behavior if her father didn't change. But some men couldn't live without cheating. They were selfish, uncaring, and refused to take responsibility for their destructive actions.

He shook his head as he relived Denny's body language and tone of voice during his confession. Not for a second did Grady believe Denny had learned how to be faithful. But he'd put on a good show of contrition. He was sure Farren had seen a similar version.

He strode into his bedroom, relived some of the exquisite moments he'd spent with Farren, then hit the shower to wash off the chlorine from the pool. Maybe he should've gone to see her immediately, but he needed to clear his head after Denny's startling confession. He wasn't sure why Denny had confided the truth, except that it bolstered the idea that he'd learned his lesson. If Denny wasn't hiding anything, then maybe Farren would trust him more easily.

But the jerk had a point about O'Hara Enterprises. Grady had been lucky these last months. Clients had understood he'd suffered a shock losing Veronica the way he had. And his agents and staff had stepped up like soldiers to handle the day-to-day. But the business was suffering from his lack of attention. Sure, he'd been online overseeing things, but it had gone on too long.

His month in New York had been a grind and more than once he'd had to take a flight. Putting out fires sometimes meant he had to be face to face. He was good at reading people, seeing what they really wanted whether that meant their ego stroked, or money saved, or to win. Video conferences were great for standard stuff, but some of his clients expected his personal attention. Now that some time had passed since Veronica's death, their patience had worn thin.

Grady stepped out of the shower to the sound of his phone pinging. And pinging again. Messages were coming in one after the other.

As he toweled off, he ran over what Farren had said about Denny. Sometimes she seemed sympathetic to him and other times, like last night when he'd been chatting and flirting with the single mom, she'd seemed wary and on alert. She hadn't liked that he'd been so engaged in the game with Mackenzie Fairfield, but Grady wasn't sure *why*. Was spending the night with Grady a form of revenge for Denny's flirting?

As soon as the thought entered his head, he called himself a fool. That wasn't Farren's style. He cursed Denny for planting the seed in the first place. But maybe Veronica had done that.

His phone pinged again. And once more.

"Who's rampaging now?" He'd spent the whole day yesterday handling business. Couldn't he have one morning to focus on his own life?

Apparently not, because the phone sounded again.

He finished drying himself and went to read his messages. A tech czar and a Russian businessman both wanted to buy the same island off the coast of North Africa. The problem was Grady had brokered a deal with a Saudi prince for the same island two days ago. And to top it off, the seller was aware of the new interest in his island.

He squeezed his eyes shut and thought. Men with egos the size of planets and overflowing bank accounts meant he'd have to handle this himself. He needed to meet with each interested party in person. And find another island or two if needed.

He picked up his phone and called the seller first.

FARREN HEARD A RAP on her door as she stepped out of the shower. Hoping it was Grady, she wrapped herself in a towel and went to answer. Looking through the peephole, she saw Eva. Hiding her disappointment, she opened the door and waved her friend inside.

"I thought it might be Grady," she said a little breathlessly.

"You answered the door in a towel?"

Heat crept up her cheeks. "I spent the night with him and when I woke, he was in the pool doing laps and chatting with some of the guests." She smiled. "It was the cutest thing. He helped Topher learn to float. I think your lesson with him will go well."

"Great!" Eva dropped her backpack to the floor and headed to Farren's small fridge with her lunch in her hand. "Grady's not in the pool now. I'd have seen him. Your friend Denny is swimming though."

"Was Mackenzie with him?"

"They were talking by the deep end, looking very connected. Why? You don't mind, do you? You're with Grady and Denny was a lot of years ago."

Hmm. She'd have to put some thought into how to handle what she knew. Maybe it wasn't her business to speak up. But asking Mackenzie a couple of questions wasn't exactly spilling Denny's secret. Torn, she covered with a smile. "No, of course I don't mind. Denny's here like any other single dad. And Mackenzie's smart."

"That's right, everyone deserves a second chance at finding love."

"Which is the whole reason for Singles Fest." She felt better. Just because Denny had screwed up badly before didn't mean he'd do it again. He claimed he'd learned his lesson and from what she saw he was putting his children first now.

Farren nodded and went to her dresser for her clothes. "Everyone who's going to Barnacle Bill's this morning is leaving at nine thirty." She looked forward to seeing if Grady remembered their conversation about stealing kisses behind the windmill. "Have you had many requests for sitters?"

"They're all booked for tonight. I'd say that means last night's dinner was a success. I may need to beat the bushes for more teens for the rest of the summer."

"Fantastic." Farren picked out shorts and a loose blouse from the closet and headed into the bathroom to change, keeping the door open so they could talk. She smoothed on her moisturizer and sunscreen. "How was your evening? I lost track of you when Grady and I got outside." She'd been focused on him and he on her. A thrill shot through her at the memory.

"I didn't actually leave the hotel," Eva said faintly.

Farren poked her head out of the bathroom door to see her friend pulling her tee off over her head. Underneath, she wore her tank suit for lifeguarding. When Eva's head popped clear of the material, Farren spoke.

"Did you stay behind with Jesse?"

"Yes." Eva's face blanked.

"But I thought you didn't want to get involved with"—oh, how to put this delicately— "someone with children?" Eva hadn't said those words exactly, but her attitude, body language and disinterested expression made it clear. Grady thought so, too.

"I don't want someone with children. But they weren't here. Jesse came without them." She bit her lip. "But I won't be seeing him again. He is definitely a package deal and..." she trailed away, her face reddening.

"And?" Farren coaxed as she stepped out of the bathroom, buttoning her blouse.

"And I don't want to talk about it." Eva spun on her heel and hurried out the door.

Stunned, Farren drifted into the room. Whatever this was with Eva, wasn't going to be fixed with a simple conversation. Not a chance. There was a whole story here and in the few months she'd known Eva,

Farren realized she hadn't scratched the surface of what made her friend tick.

She finished dressing, fully expecting a visit from Grady, but when he didn't show, she decided to check with him before starting work. A flutter in her belly did not mean she was nervous about seeing him in the bright light of day.

The wings of a thousand butterflies did not flap in her chest as she ate a very quick breakfast of an energy bar and an apple. Her ears didn't strain to hear a ping on her phone or a knock at the door as she brushed her teeth.

None of that happened. Because that would mean she was afraid of seeing him. Afraid of seeing dismissal in his eyes. The kind she'd seen before when a fling was over. Grady was different. He was real and interested. All his considerate gestures had shown her how real he was.

The business advice.

The repaired walkway.

The repainted playground.

The late-night phone calls. Even the ones from exotic places and time zones. Maybe especially those because his hours had been different. He'd been on his way to lunch, or a meeting or another airport and he'd find a way to call her when her day was done.

Her breath caught at the next one, the romantic catered dinner on the beach.

No one could fake what they'd had with each other over these weeks.

Grady was real and what they'd shared last night had been real.

And no, she wasn't nervous as she knocked on his door, and peered through the gauzy curtains with her breath held. He was taking a long time to answer. He was probably in the shower, or dressing. Or on the phone.

"HI," GRADY SAID AS he answered the door. "I was just coming to say goodbye." He bussed Farren's cheek. His suitcase sat at his feet and his laptop bag was in his hand. "I'm on the run. My plane is waiting. I have to catch a flight at JFK for Singapore, so I chartered a local to get me to New York ASAP."

"Oh!" She looked startled and blinked several times. "You're leaving." Her tone flattened and her face closed.

He'd been brusque, and not at all the doting lover. Her disappointment was written on her face.

"I'm sorry, Farren. I wish I had more time to explain, but things have blown up and I'll be on flights across the globe over the next forty-eight hours at least." He grimaced at the pace he'd have to set. "Likely longer." He kissed her lips quickly but didn't have time to pull her in for a hug. "I hope you understand. I'll text you more later."

He stepped outside and pulled the door shut behind him. "And I'll call tonight, from wherever I am. I promise." He bussed her cheek again. "Thanks for last night." He searched her eyes for a quick moment but couldn't read them. For once, Farren wore a poker face and her eyes had shuttered to dark purple, all the light gone from them.

"Sure, of course. We'll talk then." She smiled and shooed him away.

He took the hint and strode the breezeway toward the front side of the house and his car. His phone rang and when he looked it was the seller. He turned back around to see Farren, walking in the other direction, her back to him. "I'll call. I promise," he said. "I already miss you."

"Me, too." She called back without turning to face him. She lifted her phone and checked it. "It's Delphine." Farren waved goodbye over her shoulder.

He'd been dismissed. Nothing that he didn't deserve, but he didn't like the feeling. He'd upset her and would have to make it up to her as soon as he could. With Veronica and previous women that would mean a call to a jeweler. But Farren needed more than cold diamonds. Deserved more.

He stowed his bag and laptop in the car's trunk. He climbed in, started the car, and reversed out of his spot. Her little orange car sat like a pumpkin in a patch of shade.

He frowned and told his phone to call her as he drove Main Street toward the bridge.

She didn't pick up.

He tried Delphine. She didn't answer either. Great. They were comparing notes on his terrible behavior.

The seller from Singapore called again.

FARREN MET DELPHINE at Barnacle Bill's. The other woman looked distracted and upset, so as soon as Farren had ushered her group through the tentacles of the octopus that made up the gate to the park, they wandered to the tables near the snack bar.

Delphine sat while Farren went to the window to order two coffees.

"How was your evening?" Delphine asked, as Farren set the paper cups on the table.

"A roaring success," she declared. "I think Singles Fest will be a success. The clients are enjoying themselves, the kids are having a blast, and it looks like some sparks have ignited between some of the adults. Tonight is the dinner on the beach. It's fully booked and so are the babysitters."

"And you and Grady are fine?"

"Sure, of course," Farren said with a flush. Last night had been great, but the way he'd rushed off this morning had seemed dismissive. She tried to remember his promise to call later, but he'd been so preoccupied, she had to wonder.

"Because he took off first thing this morning," Delphine pointed out. She searched Farren's gaze. Looking for doubt? Insecurity? It was anyone's guess, so Farren deadpanned.

"He had to fly to Singapore and then he said he'd be crisscrossing the globe to sort out an emergency." She shrugged to indicate the sudden trip wasn't a problem. "No biggie."

Delphine shook her head and eyed her. She looked mournful and clicked her tongue sympathetically. Farren braced herself.

"This was how it was before," his sister commented. "Grady never had time to give to a woman." Delphine patted her hand. "Please try not to read anything into his leaving."

"I won't." But she'd felt a sting when he'd given her the news and she'd seen his face. He'd been distracted and brusque. His mind had been elsewhere and consumed with this new emergency.

Delphine sipped her coffee and grimaced. "This is awful."

Farren leaned in. "The counter help is Tom Fester's sister-in-law, Fiona, and she's a tea drinker."

"That explains it. Never trust a tea drinker to make a decent cup of coffee."

Farren chuckled, weak as Fiona's tea. "Tom's shown her how much coffee to use, but she reverts after a day or two. The coffee's hit and miss, but the locals don't complain. Fiona's been through a rough patch." She decided to push through with Delphine and help her get to the point. She had a reason for this visit and clearly had an agenda.

"Grady said he'd call me later and he's never forgotten. I'm sure I'll hear from him. We like to share how our days have gone." She smiled, feeling that she sounded strong and assured, even if she wasn't.

His sister nodded. "Good. If he's thinking of you while he's away, then you're ahead. That was one of the things he failed at before Veronica. He'd forget or ignore that he had a woman who was missing him. Sometimes he'd be gone for a week without checking in." She frowned. "He was never fair, never considerate. But how could he be while he was building the company?"

Farren hoped that wasn't the case this time. But old habits die hard, and Grady could fall back into the pressure of the work. Now that they'd slept together, maybe he felt the chase was behind him and he could leave Farren on a shelf. Wouldn't be the first time she'd seen a relationship sputter to an end for lack of interest.

"That's why I want to talk with you," Delphine said in a serious tone.

Finally! The point. "I was beginning to wonder," Farren responded drily.

Delphine dropped her smile and thinned her lips. Underneath, Delphine was as gruff as her brother was when they'd met. "I'd like you to consider joining O'Hara Enterprises as Grady's assistant."

Farren reared. "What?"

"You'd be a great member of his team. He needs a righthand and you're perfect. You're organized, and prompt, and detail oriented. And you're great with people. Sometimes my brother can be grating. I'm sure you noticed that when you met him."

Farren stared. "I'm not sure I'm following. You want me to leave my business? The one I've worked on for over a year? The one that looks like it'll be a screaming success?" A business that made her happy. That made *other people happy*.

She shook out her fingertips to get the blood flow back. She'd swear all her blood was leaking out of her overloaded brain. *Yes, that was it.* That's why her hands felt like ice and her mouth stopped working.

Again, his sister patted her hand as it lay like a dead fish on a dock. She looked down to see the other woman's square blunt fingers fluttering across her hand. She saw the fingers move but didn't feel them.

And suddenly, everything started moving again in a rush of sound and smells and feelings. "I can't do that. I *won't* do that." She couldn't throw herself into Grady's life. Not without an invitation.

Again with the sad face. The *concerned* face. Delphine had both down pat. "Of course you can. You've had one fun weekend with Singles Fest. But with Grady you'll have travel, and the money you'll make helping him would be more than a small business can generate. Your target market with Singles Fest is limited. People like the ones you have here"—she waved toward the laughing groups of golfers—"can't afford to pay more. And with Grady you'd have no other responsibilities."

"This was all about replacing Veronica. Not just as an assistant, but as his girlfriend." Her tone went flat as the realization took over her mind.

Delphine made a moue with her lips. "That may be how it looks, but I assure you, you're nothing like her. You're a much better match for my brother. He'll see that soon."

Veronica had been Grady's love. The woman he wanted to spend his life with. Sure, he'd admitted his feelings for her were mixed up with his business, but lots of power couples shared business responsibilities.

"I don't know if I should be grateful or insulted. You're asking me to be her replacement, *in every way*, when Grady hasn't asked me for more than what we have." With that, Farren rose from her seat and stalked toward her car. But ten steps away she turned back. She wasn't done with this yet. By thirty-four she may not have the children she assumed she would, or the loving husband she'd hoped for.

But she had her pride and her independence and soon, she'd have a thriving business giving people the lives *they* wanted. She was happy to help people build new families. She couldn't wait to get a wedding invitation from someone who'd met because of Singles Fest.

"You can't arrange your brother's life," she grated. "Or mine. I've never forced myself on anyone and I won't start now."

Not even when she loved Grady with all her heart. She'd known it as she'd watched him with Topher in the pool. Grady was everything she wanted. Everything she'd dreamed she'd have someday.

Farren burst into uncontrollable tears as Delphine stared, eyes wide and mouth snapped shut. Farren turned and marched to her car tears streaming to her chin. Appalled at her behavior, she swiped her hands across her cheeks and started the engine. She had to be anywhere but here, facing Grady's sister.

Chapter Twenty-one

ONE WEEK LATER...

"We'll talk when you get back," Farren promised Grady on the phone.

"Home," Grady clarified. "We'll talk when I get home." And that's exactly what he meant. This round of travel had beaten him and all he could think about was getting home to Farren.

"Sure." Farren's tone was breezy, distant. She was deep in the throes of offering a new Singles Fest program for a full week at the end of the month. She'd had lots of responses to a survey and the resounding answer to her question about returning to Last Chance Beach was *Yes*! The parents had made connections, their children had made friends, and everyone had had a great time over the Fourth. And they'd told their friends, so growth was a given. He couldn't be prouder of her.

Last night, she'd casually mentioned that Denny and his children were still there. It was summer break, after all. And Denny had family in the area. At least, that's how she'd explained the man's weaseling his way into her life as soon as Grady's back was turned.

He tried not to let visions of them together crash through his control, but the guy had really messed with him. Like a tick burrowing into his armpit, Denny irritated. It didn't matter that Grady told himself he was exhausted, jetlagged, and running from buyer to buyer and from island to island trying to get a deal together. The only respite he had was talking things over with Farren.

Hearing her voice, listening to her enthusiasm for Singles Fest, knowing the high she was on with her success, cheered him. His pride would not let him ask her what was happening with Denny. Or how much she was enjoying the guy's kids. Or having fun with all of them.

He couldn't lose this with her. Refused to lose her to anyone or anything.

Farren was his and he was hers, body, and soul. He hoped. But that pretty little girl in red ringlets would draw on anyone's heartstrings. Denny aside, that happy face was tough competition.

"How's your friend Denny doing with his kids? Are the boys getting along better?" He should bang his head against a wall. That would make more sense than torturing himself by asking.

"They're doing okay. They're all spending time with his parents and Denny's brother. It was awkward at first."

"Because of his divorce? They didn't like his wife?" He waited to see if she corrected his assumption or if she was still determined not to tell Denny's secret.

"They did like his wife. But I'm sure everyone will adjust." She fell silent then and he knew she was trying not to say more. He understood her now, and her silences said more than she realized. Still, the fact that she hadn't shared the truth about Denny with him, rankled. It wasn't the same as defending him, but it was too close for comfort. "Where will you be tomorrow?" she asked, changing the subject.

"Dubai for two hours." But it wasn't for a business deal. Tomorrow was personal. "And then, home."

FARREN PULLED THE PHONE from her ear and stared at the screen. Grady had disconnected without a goodbye. He'd be in Dubai tomorrow for a very brief stop and then back in New York. Not that far. Maybe he'd return to Last Chance Beach soon. Maybe.

His call had come at mid-day when she was at her busiest answering emails that couldn't be handled by her website's FAQ page. She needed to list a bunch of new Q&As on that page. The intern that Grady had lent her could handle that. He had a great attitude and loved that his ideas were taken seriously.

She made a note to make a list of the most recent questions she'd had and pass them along.

She'd been distracted throughout the call with Grady. That was the main reason they both preferred late-night calls. They could pay attention then and really talk, not just check in.

Delphine had got to her with the whole replacing Veronica thing. It had been difficult not to let on to Grady about his sister's machinations. He'd once said the Machiavelli family had nothing on Delphine. She was the world's best manipulator. Or worst, depending on what she was after.

She'd tell Grady about his sister when he came back to Last Chance Beach. That conversation shouldn't be on the phone and not when either of them were distracted by business. She'd also tell him their fake relationship was over.

She couldn't continue. Not after falling in love with him. Not after tears had streamed down her cheeks in front of his sister. Since he hadn't mentioned her outburst, she could assume Delphine had kept the teary exchange to herself.

He'd called Last Chance Beach home, but that wasn't what he'd meant. Not really. New York City was home for Grady O'Hara, and she'd be better off keeping that front and center in her heart.

Because to put any stock in thinking he was coming home to her was setting herself up for heartbreak. Falling for Grady had been the biggest mistake of her life.

When he'd left her that morning after their night together, she'd accepted that she loved him. And now, here she was, pining for a man whose life was somewhere else. Whose dreams were somewhere else.

Not just college, like Denny.

Not just back home after a vacation like the other men she'd had hopes for.

No, Grady's dreams were global. His career demanded all of him. Veronica had been his perfect match.

And there was no way a woman from a small beach town—a woman who'd never left—a woman with small ambitions—could interest a man like Grady for long. He'd said all those things himself.

So why had he insisted he was coming home?

GRADY PARKED IN FRONT of his house behind the Landseer, feeling grubby, unkempt, and unshaven. His beard itched in the summer heat, and he must smell like a bear. But he didn't want to waste a moment. He climbed out of his rental, a sedan this time, and hustled inside.

He slapped his face with cool water, let it air dry and headed to the fridge for a cold glass of water. He tipped the tumbler up and drank the whole thing down.

From the sounds of splashing and children laughing, people were in the pool. Was it Denny and his kids? If it were, he'd have a chat with him.

He stepped out of his door and caught sight of a familiar stroller. Good, he was here.

Grady halted in his tracks when he saw who was holding the little girl in the pool and making her giggle.

"Farren," he called, stunned at the image of her with the child braced on her hip. The child was in a bathing suit with an adorable sun hat on her head.

Farren whirled and faced him, her beautiful face a mask of surprise. "Grady! You're here!" Her voice sounded delighted and happy. She clutched the child to her chest and for a moment he had a glimpse of her future. Farren wanting children was a given.

Whether they'd be his was the biggest question of his life.

"O'Hara. I thought you were off globe-trotting," Denny said from the far side of the pool. He pulled himself up to sit on the edge, flanked by his two sons. Grady couldn't read the boys' expressions, but their father's was clear.

"I don't mean to interrupt," Grady said while he smiled stiffly. Farren looked startled, the way she had the first time they'd met, and his smile had been more of a snarl. Her glance darted to Denny and back again. "I wanted to say hi before I cleaned up. Care to join me for dinner Farren?"

She flushed and began to walk to the stairs to exit the pool. "I'll join you now if that's okay. We need to talk."

He nodded and watched as she rose from the pool, water streaming down her luscious curves. She lifted a towel from the stroller and wrapped the giggly child. Without another word, she strolled to where Denny sat and handed the baby to him.

The looks Denny's boys gave Farren were identical. Adoration.

Denny had been busy this week. He'd been wooing Farren and using his kids as bait, just as Grady suspected.

When Farren turned to face him, she wore the same determined look she'd had when she'd pounded on his door and barged her way into his life. She scooped up a larger towel and patted herself dry before wrapping it around her torso.

"You're right," Grady said as she reached his side. "We need to talk."

WHEN GRADY DIDN'T DRAG her into his arms for a kiss, Farren knew what was coming. His goodbye speech. His 'it's not you, it's me' speech. His 'this small town won't work for me' speech. Whatever he said, however he said it, they were at *The End*. She appreciated that he'd chosen to do this face-to-face.

Still, she followed him into his house. Once in the kitchen he waved at the fridge. "Water?"

"No, thanks." She wandered into the living room and perched on the edge of the futon; much the way she had the day they'd met.

"About Denny," he said, taking the seat next to her. She could feel his heat, see concern in his eyes. "There's something off about him. I don't trust him."

"I see." She mulled the odd direction the conversation had taken. "Denny's fine. He's just going through something right now. He's making the best of a bad situation."

"That's what you think?"

"Of course. I haven't told you everything about him, but believe me, he's trying his best to be a good father."

Defeat flickered in the back of Grady's eyes. "You'll wait while I shower and shave. I must look like a bear."

"You remind me of the first night I walked in here."

"Best night of my life," he murmured a moment before he skimmed his lips across hers. "Until the night before I left. I'm so glad to be home."

She kissed him back. How could she not? She loved him. Her tongue sought his, her arms rose to hold him close, and she sighed against his lips. "I'll wait here while you clean up. Are you hungry?"

"Starved," he admitted as he turned away. He was so big, so square, so vital. And she'd miss him.

She headed into the kitchen to prepare a sandwich. His salad fixings were wilted, but she found cheese and bread and butter. "One grilled cheese sandwich coming up," she muttered.

Before he got to his 'it's been nice, but' speech, she remembered she wanted to tell him about Delphine's suggestion. If they were going to part ways, he should know the extent of his sister's manipulations. It was the least she could do for him. That, and wish him well.

He took little time to shower and shave, but when he walked back into the kitchen, he smelled great, looked less like a bear and more like himself.

"Grilled cheese? One of my favorites."

"If I'd known you were coming home so soon, I'd have brought in fresh fruit and veggies. Your milk's okay though." She'd checked the date before she put the coffee on. "It's fine for coffee."

"I need one," he said as he settled into a chair. He wolfed down his sandwich and smiled when he was finished. "Thanks."

"About Delphine."

"About Denny."

They both smiled awkwardly.

"You first," he coaxed.

"She admitted that she wanted me to step into Veronica's shoes. A replacement. That was her plan all along. She offered me a position as your assistant."

His mouth opened and his brows knit in confusion. "I swear I had no idea. What did she say about Singles Fest?"

"That it was small time and I'm not going to grow it the way I hope to. She said the same thing you did at first. I was targeting the wrong market."

"But it makes you happy and as long as it provides a good living, it's a success. I believe Singles Fest will give you that."

She nodded. "Thank you. It means a lot to hear you say that." But there was more to say. "I could never replace Veronica. You loved her. She was the woman you wanted to spend your life with. And, frankly, I'd be second best. I can't just step into her shoes, into your bed." She bit her lower lip and gathered her courage. "I want to end this fake relationship. It's too hard for me. My feelings are complicating everything."

"No." Grady rose to his feet and took her hand to have her stand and face him. "You're not second best, Farren. You're the woman I love. The woman I want to be with forever."

HE'D SPOKEN AWKWARDLY, brokenly, as he'd realized he was in real danger of losing Farren. If he didn't do this right, Denny waited outside his door, ready to pounce. He tugged Farren close and tilted her chin up with the tip of his finger. "I love you," he repeated.

He cupped her jaw in both of his palms and kissed her gently. But Farren didn't want gentle. She slammed her body against his. Her towel dropped to the floor, and suddenly he had his hands on her warm, naked flesh. Her bathing suit was damp, but her skin—her skin was heaven. He traced her smooth, soft, back, landing below her waist. He clasped her full cheeks in his palms and squeezed lightly, bringing a moan from her.

Or maybe it was his moan that filled the kitchen.

She reared back and looked at him, her lips wet from his kisses, her eyes full of disbelief. "Really? This isn't at all what I was expecting."

"What did you think after last week? After that night. After I said I was coming home."

She shook her head. "I don't know. Not this. This is a dream."

He pinched her bottom and dragged her into hips. "This, sweet Farren, is no dream." He shuddered at the feel of her against him. "Can we take this into the bedroom? I know you said we need to talk, but I can't think with you in my arms. I've had the week from hell trying to get back here to clear the air."

She twined her fingers with his and gave him a come-hither smile that sent a pile driver from his chest to his toes. All he could manage was to follow her like a docile lamb.

Once in the bedroom, he unhooked her bathing suit top and watched it fall to the floor. Next, she bent over to pull down her bottoms. She looked at him over her shoulder with a saucy smile that enflamed him. Lifting the covers, she slipped between his sheets and waited while he undressed.

He'd never moved so fast in his life.

But once he climbed in to join her, to join *with* her, he propped his head on his hand and leaned over her. She scooched close and slid her leg over his thighs.

"Yes?" she whispered. "What can I do for you? Tell me what you need to say."

"I said something significant in the kitchen. Something that usually gets a response in a similar vein." He needed to know Farren was his and his alone. Veronica had twisted him, had made him doubt his judgement, his feelings. "The last woman I thought I loved, didn't love me."

"Grady, what are you saying?" Her hand came up to cup his ear and she shifted closer.

He had to explain himself. Farren had a right to know and deserved to understand why he'd gone to ground and stayed there. Why he'd ghosted his own sister. Why he didn't tell her he loved her before he left for Singapore.

"Veronica was on the lake that night so she could hook up with the man she really loved. They planned for us to have a short marriage and then a divorce with a high payoff."

Anger flashed behind her eyes as Farren struggled to rise. When she did, she held her head in her hands, her eyes wide and blazing on his behalf. "Oh, Grady. All this time, I thought you still loved her. That you were grieving." She heaved in a breath. "But you were *betrayed*. I believed you could never love me the way you loved her. The way I love you."

And there it was. The confirmation he'd needed. He felt like a fool to need it. A fool to want to hear the words. *Betrayed.* Yes. *Wounded.* Yes.

He'd been hounded by the doubt Veronica had infected him with. Month after month. He closed his eyes tight. "If you hadn't pushed your way into my life, I might have stayed there in that dark, angry place." He dragged in a ragged breath, but she had tears in her eyes and her lips pinched closed. He didn't want her crying for him. Because he was better now. She'd made him better.

"I couldn't talk about it," he explained hoarsely. "Not with you, not with anyone. The first few months, yes, I grieved. The circumstances of her death right before the wedding nearly undid me. And then, I heard from her lover, a man who was reeling from what he'd set in motion. He had enough information to convince me it was all true."

He could tell her now, he realized. This woman who loved him. This woman who'd brought him back to life with her sunny optimism and cheerful ways. His sprite. His love. His Farren.

He reached for her then and she came into his arms. Her love surrounded him, made him whole and gave him hope.

AFTERWARD, AS THEY snuggled under the rumpled sheets, Farren ran her foot up from Grady's ankle. His leg hair felt bristly, his body heavy and warm alongside hers. She settled her head on his shoulder and lay her arm across his chest.

"This is heaven," she murmured. She wasn't sure she'd ever fully comprehend the depth of Grady's anguish over Veronica. She'd shown him her love, given him everything he'd wanted in these last hours. Dawn was approaching and they'd spent the whole night loving and talking and loving again.

"Yes, it's heaven. When I said this was home, I meant it. I'm moving here. I want our life together to be in Last Chance Beach."

"I could move to New York with you." She could and she would if he needed to be there rather than this small beach town where nothing much happened.

He shook his head. "I love it here. I love that you love it here. I don't want to race off the way I did last week. I'm hiring more brokers in Europe and Asia. I want to be here when we have a family."

"Oh. I want that, too. So much." Her breath caught. "Denny had hopes I'd—well, that doesn't matter."

"Actually, it does," he said huskily. "As childish as it sounds, I need to know what happened with Denny."

She raised her lips and kissed his chin. And told him about Denny and his two families and the complete mess he'd made. "Of course I knew about it the day he turned up for the Fourth, but I also held onto my memories of the boy I knew, and cared deeply for, in high school. He's doing what he can to make a family out of the ashes, but I won't be the woman who helps."

"His boys seemed to like you."

"They're good kids, just angry at their father. I think they may be okay with each other given time. They're not to blame for their father's mistakes. I suggested that Denny get them into counseling. I believe he's considering it." She'd also had a brief conversation with Mackenzie Fairfield who'd quickly picked up on Denny's roving eye. The single mom had assured Farren she was looking for a keeper rather than a charmer.

Grady shifted and pulled himself up to sit with his back to the headboard. "That little girl of Denny's is a cutie." He looked at her with earnest hope. "If it's all right with you, I'd like you to give me one of those."

She laughed. "There's no red hair in my family, but I'll do my best."

"No problem, there's red in mine."

SUNDAY OF LABOR DAY weekend, Last Chance Beach

"Hurry or we'll miss it," Grady said and pulled Farren out of the lounger beside the pool. At least he wasn't yanking her arm out of its socket. The big man had no idea how powerful he was.

"This is my first moment of rest all weekend," she whined. Singles Fest was all she'd hoped for and more. "This weekend is about working people taking a day of rest and I've worked myself to the bone."

"You have," he agreed sympathetically. "But tonight's the night and I want to see it for myself."

"You're obsessed with your sister's romance. Let it be. Things will advance as they will." *Things* had moved along at a fast pace for her and Grady once they'd cleared the air about Denny and Grady decided to move to the island. She got all warm and tingly just thinking about their nights together.

While she and Grady had been fake dating, Delphine had been busy getting to know James, the chef at The Captain's Table. "Funny how neither of us wondered why she was spending so much time here when we met."

"That's how she operates," he explained again as she stepped off the lawn and onto the wooden walkway. He took her hand in his and she looked up at him, knowing that he had more to say about his twin. "She's private about her own life, while sticking her nose into mine. Do you know she wants to go ring shopping with us? She thinks I won't give you a diamond you deserve."

Farren barked a laugh. It could've been a snort, but Grady was too kind to notice those.

"Where are you taking me?"

"To the observation platform. We can see from there."

"See what?"

"Their romantic dinner." He spoke as if to a child.

"No, no, that's tomorrow night," she said, frowning. "I'm sure I booked the group dinner for then."

"I love your focus on Singles Fest but try to follow along. Think back to our first dinner on the beach."

He steered her onto the viewing platform and turned her to face the ocean. Then he cozied up behind her and held her shoulders. His mouth sat next to her ear and his breath sent tendrils of heat down her spine.

"Oh, I see," she said. And suddenly she knew how they must have looked on the night of her surprise dinner on the beach.

Two people sat kitty corner to each other, oblivious to the servers standing off to the side at a prep table filled with everything they'd need to feed the happy couple. Light from the tall lanterns cast a golden glow across Delphine's face and shoulders, giving her a nimbus worthy of an angel. Farren's heart expanded as she took in the scene. So sweet. So romantic.

So very private.

"We shouldn't be watching this," she said. "It's their moment." She blinked moisture out of her eyes when she saw James rise from his chair to kneel in front of Delphine. "It's too personal, Grady." She turned to face him.

He was on one knee, too, and in his hand was an open velvet box. She gasped. "Did Delphine shop for this?"

He shook his head. "She doesn't know you like I do."

"Oh, Grady." There, in the box, sat a deep blue square cut sapphire surrounded by diamonds that glittered like stars. "I love it."

"I can't face another week without knowing if this is real, Farren. If what we have is forever. Because that's what I want. Forever with you."

They'd spoken of their love many times. Simple words with a wealth of meaning. They'd confirmed they wanted children, where they'd live, how they'd manage his newly pared-down schedule. And still, he looked uncertain. For a man whose trust had been shattered, Grady needed to feel her love, not just hear about it.

"Oh, Grady, the fake thing was real from the start, we just didn't know it." Farren sank to the wooden planks to join him chest to chest, face to face. His arms closed around her as he set his lips to hers.

They had each other, for real, and forever.

IF YOU ENJOYED **Fake Me** and have ever found a wonderful romance by reading reviews, please pay it forward by sharing a few words about how **Fake Me** made you feel when you closed it. A review doesn't have to be long, or a retelling of the plot, just a few words on how you felt when you finished. Did you sigh at the end? Feel happy?

If you want to hear about exciting new releases and deals, please subscribe to Bonnie's Newsy Bits on my website. Readers can download a free short romance set in Last Chance Beach when they subscribe. Over 40 romance titles are listed on my website at https://www.bonnieedwards.com/.

Want more Singles Fest? **Take Me (and My Kids),** Eva and Jesse's story is available for ebook and print. **Make Me**, the story of Archie Jones and Beth Mathews will launch October 9, 2023, in ebook and print. It is available for pre-order now!

Did you know?

Last Chance Beach was created by a group of romance authors back in 2020. We wanted to have a summer place where the living was easy and the romance perfect! We're mid-series now with lots of books available and many more to come. You'll find sweet romances to steamy, a bit of suspense, blended families, there may even be a bit of spooky.

But most of all, you'll be swept away to our lovely seaside town where all the endings are happy. You can find the books already available here: https://www.amazon.com/dp/B09S3BGDZ including my title, **Fake Me.** You can also get updates and hang out with the authors and readers of the series in the exclusive Facebook Group *Last Chance Beach Romance Readers*.

Recent and Upcoming Last Chance Beach Titles

Fake Me – Aug/21 – Bonnie Edwards
Masquerade Under the Moon – Oct 2/22 – Kari Lemor
Island Treasure – Nov/22 - Susan R. Hughes
Where Dreams Come True – Dec/22 Judy Kentrus
Beating in Time - Feb/23 - MJ Schiller
You...Again – Mar/23 - Nancy Fraser
Take Vitamin Sea for Love – Jun/23 -Annee Jones
Solace Under the Stars - Jul/23 – Kari Lemor
Make Me – Oct/23 - Bonnie Edwards (available for pre-order)
Beacon of Thanks– Nov/23 – Judy Kentrus
And more in 2024!

Don't miss out!

Visit the website below and you can sign up to receive emails whenever Bonnie Edwards publishes a new book. There's no charge and no obligation.

https://books2read.com/r/B-A-JXD-EVWPB

BOOKS 2 READ

Connecting independent readers to independent writers.

Did you love *Fake Me*? Then you should read *Take Me (and My Kids)*[1] by Bonnie Edwards!

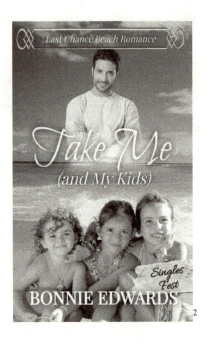

Take me, take my kids. Simple. Unless the woman of your dreams has the best reason in the world not to.

Single dad Jesse Carmichael met the perfect woman in Last Chance Beach, but when she heard about his three children, she bailed. Hard.

But Jesse has a plan.

Eva Fontaine has stepdaughters in the custody of their grandparents. She's the only mother they remember, and she moved across the country to be near them. Her life is centered on staying in their lives while avoiding handsome, caring Jesse.

---

1. https://books2read.com/u/4jgB9k

2. https://books2read.com/u/4jgB9k

Eva refuses to get involved with another single dad. Falling for Jesse means loving his children. She's done that once and her heart can't take another beating if she should lose them, too.

But Jesse has a new plan to help her and desperate Eva's onboard with it.

Until his children throw another insurmountable obstacle in their paths.

Now, Jesse has a plan for that, too.

At Last Chance Beach love takes a stand...

About the Author

Bonnie Edwards has been published by Kensington Books, Harlequin Books, Carina Press, and more.

With over 40 titles to her credit, her romances have been translated into several languages. Her books are sold worldwide.

Learn about more exciting releases and get a **free** romance by subscribing to her newsletter, **Bonnie's Newsy Bits** through her website.

https://www.bonnieedwards.com/

Cheers and happy reading!

Bonnie Edwards

CPSIA information can be obtained
at www.ICGtesting.com
Printed in the USA
LVHW041143030523
745942LV00001B/27